RIVERFRONT DREAMS

RIVERFRONT DREAMS

A novel by

Daniel Isaac Morris

VICOA.COM
Pennsylvania, USA

ISBN-10 0982825048
ISBN-13 9780982825044
Published by Vicoa.com

Be sure to read *Grave Creek Connections*,
the book that precedes this one.

Other Morris books are:

Swaypole, a tale of mystery, populated with little people, carnies, ex-spies and mafia dons. The tale of intrigue is set in the mythical town of Gibsonton, WV

Cheat River, at the head of the Cheat is a plot that is too horrible to contemplate.

didyahavadaddy, a humorous look at the other side of public school education.

Grave Creek Connections, a murderous cult operates among the citizens of a small Pennsylvania town.

Grave Creek Conspiracy, Eden Whitloe tries to solve "The Beautiful Maidens Murders" while a secret cult tries to keep its secrets and the murders from being discovered.

Available on line or at your favorite book store.

Be sure to visit http://www.dimorris.com

For the Morris, Rogers, Lambert and Kincaid Families.

For Barbara, Danny, Keli, Neil & Kelley
Webster and the late Ben Bird

Daniel Isaac Morris

Prologue

The author is a member of two Home Owners' Associations (HOAs). Both are relatively benign. *This novel is a work of fiction and is not at all about them.* That said, HOAs are, arguably the nation's most powerful civic governance bodies and some of the abuses mentioned in this book are from current headlines. Moreover, the tribulations they and their residents encounter are numerous and ongoing—the material of legend. This is not an attempt at an exposé. All of this stuff is well known, but perhaps any future homeowners should exercise caution. *Caveat emptor*—particularly when purchasing this book.

Each year at the end of January, Ye Mystic Krewe of Gasparilla invades the City of Tampa, Florida as they have been doing since 1904. You are invited to join the fun of the 'Pirate Fest' before and after the invasion, where fun will be had by all. Get on board with the swashbucklers before your swash begins to buckle.

Chapter 1

Okay, so it's not as spectacularly beautiful as the Elfin River—sorry—the Elfin is now called the Dora Canal. To me, the Elfin River has a better ring to it. The Ocklawaha is big and wide in some places; it's narrow and dredged in others. It has been abused beyond the environmentalists' worst nightmare, but it still has its moments, its scenic spots, where live oaks dip their Spanish moss in its now murky waters.

The Dora is impressive in its primordial splendor; the canal is stunning but short. Upon entering the canal one fully expects to see a brachiosaur stick his long neck between the ancient bald cypress trees that line the waterway. Birds screech out jungle-like sounds in an African-like setting. The Dora is such a stand-in for an African river; retakes for *The African Queen* were filmed here. However, a brief passage from Lake Eustis to Dora Lake and the one and a quarter mile trip brings boaters back to the reality of what Florida has become. This is to say it has become a different place, leaving old Crackers as strangers in a strange land.

It's as if the Ocklawaha was punished for its role as a

waterway for steamboats that transported citrus, lumber, sea island cotton, sugar, and other agricultural commodities to ports on the St. Johns River. The Ocklawaha is now what Florida has become.

In some respects the river has taken on many aspects of a Christ-like redeemer who absorbs the sins of the river's surroundings and takes them for itself.

For its participation in the citrus industry it was 'rewarded' with the pollution provided by fertilizer runoff from the groves. For its participation in the commerce of Florida, it was 'rewarded' by its inclusion in the ill-conceived and ill-fated Cross-Florida Barge Canal. Fortunately more intelligent politicians prevailed in that case and the canal project was abandoned.

Dammed, dredged, polluted, and abused, the Ocklawaha endures and tries to reassume some of the beauty of the Old Florida days. As the old song goes, "That Old Man River keeps rolling along," contributing what it can to the rich ecology of the region. With a little imagination, one can envision a wooden steamboat plying a pristine river under a canopy of water oaks and cypresses draped with moss while alligators and turtles patrol the shores. You needn't imagine the ibis or heron swooping across the bow, or the osprey that soars overhead—they never left.

* * * *

In a very small inlet just south of the Highway 42 Bridge, Jake Summerfield and Denny Denhart were trying to negotiate their boat into fresh fishing grounds. The men were nearly twins—fraternal twins—because their faces looked nothing alike.

They were from solid 'Florida Cracker' stock, tanned where their skin was exposed, but white where they had the good sense to keep it protected from the damaging sun that was the trademark of their home state. They intuitively knew what few tourists did.

The term 'Cracker' is not a derogatory term for many Floridians. It is a term filled with pride. Crackers are too self-reliant and independent to need everything that development brings. There are all sorts of ideas about the origin of the term 'Cracker', none are very definitive.

Eventually the canopy enveloped them, closed over them and seemed to tighten around their small skiff.

"Maybe we oughta' forget it for today and come back with the canoe. It's getting' real tight in here," said Jake.

The narrow inlet closed in and now seemed more like a room than a hallway. Midges—the blind mosquitoes of the region— swarmed in front of Denny who didn't seem to notice their annoying presence. He knew they didn't bite but he could swear some biters were hanging out in their midst. The annoying little bugs just hung in the air making it seem the men would inhale them. They hummed in Jake's ears as he fanned a path through them with his hat, then he stopped and stooped to look through the branches of the small trees and bushes surrounding them.

There was water ahead, water behind and on both sides, but they could no longer make forward progress. Off to the left there was a pig-like grunt; a noise Denny recognized as one of a number of a gator sounds.

"Sounds like a big fella," Jake said.

"Hope he doesn't want to head out over top of us," replied Denny. "You didn't leave that stringer hanging over the side, did you?"

"Might as well get outta here, couldn't get a line in the water with all this brush anyway."

Jake, who sat in the stern of the small skiff shifted the trolling motor into reverse and they started to ease their way out of what seemed like an emerald cave. Suddenly there was a thump and a whine as the motor hit something and the propeller drive snapped, freeing the motor and allowing the shaft to spin unimpeded by the prop.

Hardly missing a beat, Denny picked up an oar and started poling the boat backward toward the opening to the river.

"What the… what the' hell is that?"

"What? What-ja see?" asked Jake.

"Gotta' be a bleached out turtle shell or cow skull or something."

"Can you reach it? Pick it up."

"I ain't pickin' the damned thing up. You want it, you pick it up."

Denny poked at it with the oar. It was lodged in some trees just beyond his reach. He tried to put the oar blade over the top of it to drag it closer.

"Bigger than a softball, smaller than a soccer ball, 'bout the size of a human head," he said.

"Denny, if yer trying to make me nervous, you're doing a good job of it. The darned thing has to be a turtle shell or maybe it's one of those floats they use to mark shallow water."

"If that's what it is, it wasn't placed very good, or it's been moved. We done been in the shallowest piece of this part of the river and have a broken prop to prove it."

"Leave the danged thing there and let's get moving on out of here," complained Jake.

"I almost got it. You still got that little gaff hook? Hand it up here if you do."

Jake handed Denny the gaff and Denny pulled the object closer with the oar until he could hook it with the gaff.

Chapter 2

It seemed as if fall came earlier and earlier after Kenneth Piccard retired from Rainelle University. Summer hadn't fulfilled its promise of three or four months of balmy, or even hot weather. Could it be Al Gore was wrong? Could it be that global warming was, as Glenn Beck proclaimed, just a big scam? April had brought showers, but in the earliest part of the month, April brought spitting snow and frost-covered windshields; only later did the chilling rains that stunted the new growth of spring become reasonably warmer. It wasn't until late July that the promise of hot weather was delivered, the chill surrendered and the dog days of summer convinced folks to become Gore disciples once again. (Later, environmentalists proclaimed that global warming was as dead as global cooling had been and moved for the all inclusive and unchallengeable "climate change.")

Ken moved from Dillweed, Virginia with his parents in the 1940s and grew up on a farm in Southwestern, Pennsylvania. His daddy believed the boy was better off in small town America that is what they were used to. Dillweed was anything but a metropolis. Rainelle, Pennsylvania was a bit larger, but still nothing to write home about. It retained its 1950s small-town character well into the 21st Century.

Ken grew up, graduated from high school and attended nearby West Virginia University. When he earned his bachelor's degree, he couldn't find suitable employment so he ventured on to graduate school. He taught part-time in one of the local school districts until a Rainelle College professor's unexpected demise; he was killed in a home invasion. He volunteered to take over the late professor's classes and was eventually hired to fill the unforeseen vacancy. So it was that Ken eventually married one of his older students and the couple settled into a small-town college existence.

Unlike the stereotypical professor's wife—'Martha'—in *Who's Afraid of Virginia Woolf?* —Kenneth's wife Rayna seldom complained about anything—to Ken. However, more recently, she began to mention the weather in more disparaging terms.

Ken *was* the stereotypical professor husband. He could have stood in for George in *Whose Afraid of Virginia Woolf* if Richard Burton were indisposed. Finally, it was too hot for a sport coat or cardigan so Geor… Ken was in more comfortable attire. A T-shirt emblazoned with 'I'm with Butt Head,' which didn't amuse Rayna at all, sweat pants with bleach splotches and leather deck shoes, sans socks, were his choices of the day.

Rayna considered herself a notch above the herd, attractive in a frumpy sort of way and with a personality and demeanor that was very average and also frumpy. Bleached blonde hair, pants with stirrups, revealing a flat, un-creased camel toe, a frilly blouse displaying a muffin rack of some size but not large enough for melons and too much make-up made her a minimal threat to the professors' wives' happy homes.

Rayna would have you believe she was *avant-garde*, chic to a fault but her tastes ran more to Miller Lite than Dom Perignon.

It isn't as if Southwestern Pennsylvania is plagued with arctic winds and indiscriminate blizzards, its climate might be described as a bit cooler than moderate. Rainelle had its hot and humid days and during those times Ken and Rayna escaped to their summer camp in the hills of West Virginia, or took a trip to Boone, North Carolina.

Boone acquired its name from the legendary Daniel Boone, who it is claimed, used the town as a campsite. For its residents and visitors Boone is a four-season playground for sports and outdoor activities. If you can call a place to bed down overnight camping, one might suppose Boone was still a campsite. For Rayna and Ken, Boone is a one-season get-away for those seeking cool mountain breezes and 'touristy' stuff. The main attraction for the Piccards was Boone's average summer temperature of 76°F.

It was in Boone, in a café on River's street that they overheard a discussion of The Villages, an upscale retirement community in mid Florida.

"It's really nice," said Jane Cole to her friend Donna

Glaser, and that's how it all began.

Before long Rayna boldly broke into the conversation, introduced herself and began asking questions. Within a matter of minutes Kenneth was drawn into the trio and insisted on ordering an after-lunch libation for the women.

Jane assured the group she knew about The Villages from a DVD the developers of the property had sent her. "It described the place in a lot of detail," she said as Rayna slipped her arm behind her, resting it on the top of the booth. "They don't tell you much about home prices, but the community is kind of like an adult Disney World, lots of golf, other activities and lots of things to do. They even have a polo field."

"Yeah," began Donna, "it's over in the middle of the state, far away from salt water, so you don't have to worry about hurricane flooding and beach traffic. There really isn't much waterfront there; they rely on golf and other sports for entertainment. All kinds of activities and music on the village squares every evening—dancing too. They built their last community to have the look and feel of Key West. Ain't that right Jane?" She didn't wait for an answer. "It has a great small-town street ambiance if that's your thing. It's just about anything you'd want, and everything's warm and green most of the time. It's not tropical and they get an occasional frost from time to time, but compared to upstate New York, it must be heaven. Got their own schools, fire departments, the whole magilla."

"Are you thinking of going there to live?" asked Ken.

"Not really," replied Donna, "it's just that a lot of our friends live there in the winter and then come to Boone or Banner Elk for the summer. It makes for a really nice life, warm in the winter and cool in the summer."

They discussed the attractions of central Florida and the advantages and disadvantages of the area. Donna and Jane agreed that south Florida was too hot and the northern part was too cold in the winter, but that the middle was just right—sort of like Goldie Locks' soup.

* * * *

Donna and Jane were off for shopping for birdhouses at some factory outlet, leaving Ken and Rayna sitting side-by-side in the booth. Ken moved to the other bench and faced Rayna.

"Are you seriously thinking of retiring to Florida?" asked Rayna.

"I don't know about the serious part yet, but it *is* something to think about. What do *you* think?"

"There's just too, too much to consider. Family, friends, new doctors, changing registrations on cars, finding attorneys, accountants—you name it. It's a big step."

"Well," Ken said, leaning back and putting his hands behind his head, "I'm not suggesting anything for right now, but we might think about a vacation down that way. You know, look around, see what's there, check out the lay of the land. We never have seen Epcot or Disney World."

"I'm not sold on it, mind you, but I like the vacation idea."

"I thought you liked the beach. Remember when we went

to Myrtle Beach?"

"Yeah, just like every other redneck from our neck of
the woods. People go there out of force of habit more than
anything else. Miniature golf, shopping, eating and walking in
sand. Any tourist beach is a strip of sand separated by resorts
and water. The water part has tar balls, hypodermic needles,
jellyfish, rip currents and things that bite. The sand part has
tar balls, needles and half-naked, drunken teenagers throwing
missiles. Back at the resorts there are drunks, balcony diving,
stalkers, dope dealers and—

"Guess you aren't a beach sort of person. Sounds like
central Florida might be your cup of tea," offered Ken.

"Ken, I know that anywhere we go in Florida there is going
to be traffic; lots of it around Orlando or Tampa, but the central
part has to be a little bit less congested. I know Bill Michaels
who lives down in Boca Raton says he can't even get out of his
driveway in the afternoon."

"I say we go back to the motel and surf the net. Check out
some vacation packages down that way and take a look at The
Villages website."

"Okay, but we sure aren't going down there now. You can
if you want to, but I like it right here, or further north during
the summer. If I want that kind of heat, I'll find a sauna."

Chapter 3

That November, just at the end of the hurricane season, somehow Kenneth and Rayna Piccard found themselves in Rayna's brother's Dodge Caravan headed south on Route 19 traveling through West Virginia on what some wags call the "Hillbilly Highway."

They were approaching Summersville, West Virginia nearing what has been called the World's Largest Speed Trap.

"Slow down, Ken," cautioned Rayna. This area of the road is designed for fining out-of-staters. The speed limit changes several times through here, so the less than conscious outlander gets snagged more easily."

"I know, I know, we've been down this road dozens of times. We can't afford to be stopped, we have to be in South Carolina by evening. I have a motel room reserved there."

"I wish we could have taken a plane, but I can see how we are going to save money—without a car rental and all. The trip is a real bitch though, compared to a brief plane ride."

* * * *

Somewhere between North Carolina and South Carolina,

the couple saw their first glimpses of Spanish moss and cabbage or Sabal palms. Later that evening they pulled off of I-26 near Orangeburg, South Carolina with the intention of dropping down to I-95 the next morning. Ken had made reservations by way of the Internet for a one-night stay at the Southern Comfort Motel, complete with Sabal palms in the courtyard.

* * * *

"You know," said Rayna over dinner that evening, "that Interstate out there is beginning to get on my nerves. It bores me to death and we have trailer trucks up our ass at every move. Is there any way we can get to the part of Florida we are interested in other than by way of I-95?"

"I know what you're gonna' say but everybody from up north goes down I-95 into the Atlantic coast of Florida. Everyone at the university claims that's the only way to go."

"There you go again, following the herd. Didn't you ever hear of the road not taken?"

"Told-ja' I knew what you were gonna' say. Hey, I'll take a look at the map when we get back to the motel. I'm pretty sure we can catch U.S. 301 out of here and it will take us cross-country as far as Ocala anyway. There's a lot of four-lane and we can make time almost as good as the Interstate—if you don't manage to stop at every junk shop between here and there."

"There aren't as many rest stops either. What do you do if you're going through a peanut patch and have to go?"

"Mickey Dees, my fine lady, Mickey Dees. You ever hear of a wide spot in the road that didn't have one?"

*   *   *   *

Fortunately for Ken and Rayna, the Route 301 leg of their journey could be traveled easily in one day and they would not have need for one of the motels that dotted the byway. 301 used to be the major route south and literally dozens of motels were built to accommodate the thousands of southbound tourists before the Interstate system made them obsolete. A few refurbished 'motor courts' survived, but many were either razed or transformed into Chinese restaurants, dance studios, churches or still stood as shells of their former mid-priced grandeur.

'Back in The Day' billboards lined the highway indicating the distance to the next Stuckeys—an orange-roofed purveyor of pecan pralines and other stuff sold to passers-by. Other billboards advertised "See Rock City," a tourist trap in Tennessee where visitors could see seven states from atop Lookout Mountain. Evidently no one ever asked why they would think people would turn around and head back to the land of Davy Crockett, interrupting their trip to the wonders of *Tierra de la sol*.

Ken and Rayna passed by the remnants of pre-Interstate America just the way the millions of tourists on the Interstate were doing today. Rayna always said they should make a book of photographs of the way things used to be, but they never did. Ken could hear the kids saying, "But that was then, this is now." Anything that didn't have a screen or a headset was too, too passé, and deserved a by-pass.

"'Loo'duh-wi'-see' said Rayna.

"What?"

"Just reading a sign that says Ludiwici is ahead. What the heck is a Ludiwici?"

"Oh that's a little town up the road a ways. Made quite a reputation for itself back when these restaurants and motels were booming. They had the speed trap to end all speed traps in Ludiwici back then.

"During the '50s it became known as the site of a rigged up stop light that would trap motorists by changing without warning.

"The locals made *beau coup* bucks writing tickets on the thing. It made national news, and even the governor told people to avoid the town. Well, that was then, this is now," said Ken as he emphasized 'now' by pointing to a defunct business property alongside the road.

"You know how politicians refer to the non-urban areas as flyover land? This is the epitome of by-pass land. Think of all the communities that are bypassed in America. Think of all the bleeding hearts who go down I-95 in their Beemers and never give a thought to this part of the country," said Ken.

"Or its people," said Rayna

* * * *

The Florida state line, really the St. Mary's River, was just ahead. A sign proclaimed they had arrived, but that was about it. On the right was a big empty lot where the welcome center had been—'back in the day.' No tasty orange juice sample or smiling greeter, no manicured grass or sheltering palms, just weeds growing through the lot, detritus and decay. Further south were a few feeble attempts to lure the paucity of visitors that had ventured down the road less traveled, a few small-town-America small towns.

"We're coming up on Starke," mused Ken.

"So?"

"Don't get excited, the state prison is just over that way, to the west. It's interesting because Florida is serious about the death penalty—deadly serious. They execute at least one prisoner a year. In 1984 they did eight of them. Missed only one year, 2007 with no dead men walking since the death penalty was reinstated in '74. You would have thought they would have made up a case and toasted someone just to keep the record going," said Ken.

"How is it you know about this death penalty crap anyway? You never get to work that stuff into Trivial Pursuit."

"I read a book about it a few months back—maybe saw it in a magazine. Can't remember."

Over an hour later: Off to the east about two miles, a huge landing strip, long enough for a jet liner. Also unseen was the owner's home and the jet planes sitting in the driveway. They had finally arrived—FLORIDA—a land where the rich and famous settle to avoid the tax-and-spend folks in the north.

* * * *

By big city standards Ocala isn't much. Its fame rests on

the fact it was not only the home of the jet-set homeowner, John Travolta, but also, it was on the outskirts of the first Florida tourist attraction for the Piccards—Silver Springs!

Silver Springs suffered from the I-95, get-me-to-Disney-quickly—syndrome. Snake handler Ross Allen was long gone as was the first swinger, Tarzan, replaced by major acts such as Foghat and Blue Oyster Cult. Glass-bottomed barges still cruised the springs that somehow, still churned out 99.8 percent pure water while folks stared back through the bottom at curious bluegill and carp.

The kitsch of 'back in the day' was replaced by a genuine theme park complete with theme park rides, shows and the kitsch of *la Nueva Florida*.

Chapter 4

"Wanna' hang around Ocala for a while, take a Lost River Voyage or a Glass Bottom Boat ride?" Ken asked Rayna.

"You're kidding, right? Next thing you'll want to watch an alligator wrestling show. I want to get down to Orlando and check into a comfortable, real-life *resort* hotel, get a decent dinner and rest up to see some sights," complained Rayna.

"Hey, we came down here to let loose, have some fun, see how the other half lives—know what I'm sayin'?"

"Yeah, that's exactly why I want to get to Orlando sometime this evening."

*   *   *   *

South of Ocala, on a whim, Ken turned onto Route 441, which turned into Route 27.

"Over there, there it is; right under that funny looking overpass."

"That's a bridge for golf carts to pass over the highway. What's over there?" asked Rayna

"See the sign? That's the sales office for The Villages over there. That's where you can buy your retirement dream. Do you want me to pull in and stop for a look-see?"

"Not now, we'll stop on the way back, or if we get bored in Orlando, we'll make reservations to stay overnight and take a tour. I'm tired, let's get on with it," complained Rayna.

* * * *

They went through Leesburg, and followed Route 27 south, which turned off onto Route 192. Now they were into the high-speed rat race that was Mouse World Central. The closer they got, the more crowded it became and the speed increase made Ken long for the good old days of Ludowici.

"What the' hell," began Rayna, "The sign says 'Celebration' what does that mean? I thought we were in Orlando."

"It's a housing development, sort of like The Villages only more upscale, I think," said Ken as they continued through a community that looked as if it were stamped from an architectural handbook.

"You think we are going to find our motel in all this mess?" asked Rayna.

"I'm so whipped, I'm not even going to try. I'm gonna' pull into the first franchise deal I recognize, we'll get a good night's sleep and find the place where I made reservations tomorrow."

Rayna pulled up the GPS on her multi-function cell phone, pushed things around on the screen and announced, "Turn left at the next intersection. We ain't stayin' in any Norman Bates motel tonight."

* * * *

A day of pixie dust, piratical yo-hoing and small worlding
was enough for Rayna. So, they moved ever onward to the land
of the future and a showcase of global stuff where they burned
up another day and a few hundred bucks.

Next, lights, camera action and the glamour of show
business were lost on the pooped out Ken. The wild adventure
in an animal world the next day was lost in a steady drizzle of
Florida 'sunshine.'

All of this and they still hadn't experienced: SeaWorld®,
Universal Orlando®, Arabian Nights, an Ultimate Airboat Tour,
Busch Gardens, Cirque du Soleil, a Daytona 500 Experience,
Fantasy of Flight, Florida EcoSafaris, Gatorland, a Helicopter
Tour, Kennedy Space Center, Medieval Times Dinner and
Tournament, Orlando Balloon Rides, the Outta Control Magic-
Comedy Dinner Show, Pirates Cove Adventure Golf, Pirates
Dinner Adventure, the Richard Petty Driving Experience,
Ripley's Believe It or Not! - Orlando Odditorium or Sammy
Duvall's Watersports Center, SkyVenture Orlando, Sleuth's
Mystery Dinner Show, The Holy Land Experience, the Titanic
Experience, Treasure Tavern, Wet 'n Wild or something called
WonderWorks.

After a day of talking to the animals and enjoying the
autumn drizzle, Rayna and Ken retired to their water-view,
piratically themed, Caribbean, two hundred and fifty dollar a
night one-room 'suite.'

"Let's get the hell out of here," mumbled Rayna.

"Hey, you're thinking out loud."

"You with me or not?"

"I'm too tired to pack"

"I think that's the plan. They and I do mean 'they'—I think it's a conspiracy, 'they' get you down here and by the time you run through all this mess, you're too pooped to pack up and escape," opined Rayna.

"It's a conspiracy all right. A money milking scheme. I figure we paid somewhere around sixteen hundred for lodging and food and probably close to that again for entrance fees to what turned out to be elaborate Carney tourist traps. We aren't poverty stricken, but we sure as hell can't afford to stay around here much longer."

"Want to head south or north?"

"I'm ready to go look for that retirement wonderland we heard about."

"Works for me. Let's pack."

Chapter 5

One hundred and thirteen miles north of Orlando and two years earlier, in Gainesville, Louis DeVecchio and Johnny Stompanato met in a poolroom just off of South Main Street. The two had been released from the Florida State Prison near Starke, a couple of weeks apart. Their transgressions were minor compared to some, not enough for network news, but dire enough for both of them to have spent three years apiece in the slammer. If the system had been aware of some of the heavier transgressions, both men would have joined their fellow inmates on death row.

"What took so long? I been waiting for days. Thought you were supposed to get out the day after I did," complained Johnny.

"They said my papers was screwed up. Hey, what am I gonna' do, sue 'em? I was lucky to get out when I did. So you made your Earliest Possible Release Date and I didn't, so hate me."

"So where we go from here? I got enough to get by for a week or two, but it ain't gonna' last long," said Johnny.

"Hey, you're the one with the big brain, you tell me."

"You're smart enough to know I always got something lined up. I've been workin' on it, I've been workin' on it," Johnny assured Louis.

Johnny was the big brain and Louis' brain was like the Grinch's heart, about three sizes too small. Louis' I.Q. hovered somewhere around his age which was forty-two. But that made him a perfect partner for Johnny who liked to run things. On the other hand, Louis preferred to let Johnny do the heavy mental work because too much thinking made his brain hurt.

Johnny explained he needed some seed money that they would acquire by robbing a few convenience stores on their way to Ocklawaha. Once there, they would lie low for a while before they made their next move.

"I know that place," said Louis, demonstrating a rare flash of intelligence. "I heard about that in a movie or sumthin'. It's where the Ma Barker gang shot it out with the feds back in the '30s, I think it was."

"Hey, check the big brain on Louis. You can't remember to zip your fly, but you can remember shit like that."

"I remember gangster stuff, not the gangsta—Snoop Dogg, Biggie Small—crap of today, but the good old Bonnie and Clyde, Baby Face Nelson kind of gangsters. Them musta' been the good old days."

"I see your point. Johnny Dillinger was cool, not just because his name was Johnny either, mind you."

"Yeah, they say Ma Barker died with a tommy gun in her arms. Now that was cool."

"That Louis, my mind-midget friend is a load of crap, bull shit made up for suckers. If it happened, it was a plant made up to take the heat off of the guys who shot her ass up. Imagine that old lady, lookin' like your granny shot up like Swiss cheese."

Johnny and Louis grew up in the mean streets of the northeast and both had wound up in Florida because their parents had toured the Sunshine State in the early 80's. Their early adventures had left both with a longing for the sunshine way of life. They went their separate ways until meeting up at a flea market in Waldo, Florida where both were trying to sell hot jewelry they acquired in a recent burglaries.

A plain clothes state trooper, serving a tour of duty intended to stop the sale of stolen goods at flea markets, happened upon the two just as they were about to unload their ill-gotten treasures on Edna Purdy of Toledo, Ohio. From there it was a familiar story of arrest, trial and incarceration. The pair might have gotten off with lighter sentences but both had a long rap sheet and a penchant for violence which they thought added spice and interest to their résumé of activities and to their reps as bad asses.

They had no idea how to earn a living and aside from petty larceny and often more felonious crimes, they lacked the most basic of survival skills. If Louis had known how to set an alarm clock he might have made a dandy landscape laborer. He could run a wheelbarrow with the best of them. Johnny, not so much. He knew the basics of how to get to a job, but not a clue how to stay at one.

Louis and Johnny found a reasonably nice trailer not too far from Ma Barker's Hideaway—not the real hideaway, that was down on Lake Weir, a few blocks away. This particular hideaway was a bar that had taken on the fame of the name.

Ocklawaha isn't much more than a wide spot in the road where fisherman and boaters stop for supplies and tourists looking for 'Old Florida' stop and eat at Gator Joe's. The town had two 1930s claims to fame, Ma Barker and a huge gator that prowled Lake Weir. The stuffed gator now sits quietly in the front yard of Gator Joe's eatery, a place famous for Florida food. Children often stretch out on the stuffed gator posing for family pictures. Ma Barker is stretched out next to her husband Herman in Welch, Oklahoma.

To the east, strangely enough for the urban sprawl of Florida, there isn't much between where Louis and Johnny holed up and the Atlantic beaches. They weren't all that much closer to the Gulf coast either but there was more sprawl between them and the Gulf coast. And, within just fifteen miles, more or less, was an exercise in more densely packed humanity, The Villages.

"We have more than a few bucks to hold us for a while, but not enough for a lifetime of leisure in Ocklawaha," observed Louis.

"I'm workin' on it, I'm workin' on it," said Johnny.

"Glad you're the brain an' not me. I thought about it for a while, but it makes my head hurt, so I quit. Let me know when you come up with something though."

"Met this guy up in Starke, said he knew about some worthless land over on the Ocklawaha River. It was a fish camp before it was turned into a trailer park in the '80s then in the '90s it turned into nuthin'."

"We already got plenty of nuthin', that ain't helping us any."

"I was thinking, we could use what we stole for a down payment, borrow some money and build one of those retirement resorts that's so popular around here."

"Too many of them, I think," offered Louis. "Over at The Villages they're having to hustle to keep that thing going. Real estate is just too hard to unload right now."

"Yeah, but we'd have something the Villages don't."

"Yeah, a whole lot of debt."

"No you bozo. We'd have that magic real estate commodity of Florida—waterfront. If I had land that didn't have it, I'd stomp a hole in the front yard, piss in it and call it waterfront. The Villages has some, but it's a kind of swamp they made into a sort of lake. People over there will go out and spend a quarter of a million for an old trailer on waterfront property so they have a place to party on weekends and a dock for their boat. It sounds funny, but it's cheaper than renting a covered slip in some marina."

Johnny wasted the next twenty minutes explaining the Stompanato version of high finance to Louis. Although the seminal concepts were lost on Louis and not very well understood by Johnny, both were convinced they could make some serious money if they invested heavily in the real estate by the river.

"Where you gonna' find somebody dumb enough to lend us the kind of gelt it's gonna' take to do something like this?" asked the somewhat bewildered Louis.

Again, Johnny wasted the next twenty minutes explaining high finance to Louis. He explained that he knew a guy who had a very large surplus of cash—a narcotics entrepreneur—who could be approached. Johnny explained the approach would be an offer to run the cash through a legitimate real estate development business so when it came out the other end, it would be taxable profits rather than tainted drug money.

Johnny knew it was more complicated than that, but why burden Louis with particulars like hiring shady accountants, using illegal alien labor and short-changing contractors to mention only a few of the more burdensome details. Admittedly they would have to put their larcenous skills and abilities as hit men to the test from time to time, but it would all work out.

Louis and Johnny planned not to have to do much, just hire the right people, make sure the planning and work was done, apply some muscle once in a while, bust a cap on the uncooperative, bribe the right officials, and collect. Their drug selling sugar daddy would keep the skids in Tallahassee greased and it would be smooth sailing. Almost overnight the pair became 'respectable' businessmen and they were convinced they were no different than other Florida real estate developers and, in many cases, they weren't.

Within the next couple of years they were living large in a huge lakefront mansion on Lake Griffin, complete with a huge screened-in swimming pool, servants and a chauffeur they seldom used. Tied at the dock on the lake side of their new home was the hallmark of lakefront success, a Donzi runabout.

Out on Route 27/441 there were now three sales offices located in strip malls from Belleview to Leesburg. Under a huge, intricately designed cartouche with the logo, 'Riverfront Dreams,' each had a sign offering riverfront and river view homes and building lots.

The subtle differences between waterfront, water view and water access were often lost on recently retired snowbirds from the north but the differences were significant. Waterfront means the home or lot is actually on the river or lake. Water view means you can actually see some water from a window, or portion of a window of the house. Of course water access means you have the right to get to the water at some point on the property. Waterfront, very expensive, water view somewhat cheaper and water access, depending on the distance to the access, not so much.

Johnny and Louis stayed away from sales as much as possible. Johnny wasn't interested in communing with the suckers and Louis tended to wander off topic by letting too much out of the bag. It would be an unusual day of filling in for an absent employee that would find one or both of them in a sales office.

*   *   *   *

It was about this time that Rayna and Ken were checking out of their water-view piratically themed, Caribbean, two hundred and fifty dollar a night one-room 'suite.'

"Have a nice day," said the clerk in a British/Indian accent.

"You can keep your nice day," he replied. "I just want out of Orlando."

In the car, Ken asked Rayna if she would like to stop at some of the attractions between Orlando and The Villages.

"There's that tower thingy in Clermont that we passed on the way down," he offered.

No answer.

"There's the Hall of the Presidents."

No answer.

"I'm taking that as, you don't want to stop at any tourist traps on the way to The Villages."

"We might stop for some extra-strength headache tablets, but you have the idea."

"I did make reservations for "The Tour" when we get there," offered Ken.

"Good," said Rayna, absently.

"Made reservations at the River Front Inn."

"That's nice."

"Not on a river though, it's on a sort of man-made lake."

"Oh?"

"All image, never mind the truth. They made the lake out of

38

a swamp I think. Hundred and twenty-five a night."

"It's better than Orlando—price-wise—that is. Wake me when we get there. I saw all the scenery on the way down."

"You can stay right in the development, but I thought that might make it uncomfortable in dealing with them. I don't want to feel like I owe anyone anything."

"Good thinking Ken! Now shut up and let me take a nap."

Chapter 6

Things went pretty much according to plan. Rayna bitched about every feature and advantage of the particular Village they toured. When they finally decided on a 'unit' the price was far beyond what they could afford. What they *could* afford was over-priced and according to Rayna's sensibilities, shoddy.

"We have some very nice, previously enjoyed, manufactured homes in the older section," said their sales associate Beyonce Hughes.

"That's a used double-wide trailer," said Rayna in an aside to Ken, while the associate grimaced.

"Not a riverfront?" offered Ken innocently.

"You might see some water in the street when it rains, but no, it's not a riverfront. Look folks, I think we are wasting all our time here; I don't think we offer the kind of lifestyle at a price that is within your budget," announced Beyonce who was trained to be far more gracious and diplomatic than she was becoming.

What her trainer didn't tell her was that heaping helpings of patience and forbearance are limited quantities in high-pressure real estate dealings. And there are more suck... er-customers waiting for the next tour.

"That bitch's name isn't Beyonce," offered Rayna as they left. "She picked that off of MTV for name recognition and—."

"Yes dear, hold it down and let's make sure we are out of ear shot before you start pissing off everyone and we have to find our own way out of here."

"A used trailer eww."

* * * *

"Heard yinz talkin' back there," said a guy who seemed to have sneaked up behind them and appeared out of nowhere.

"The world could hear us talking; a deaf man could hear us—who the hell are *you*?" asked Ken.

"Permit me to introduce myself," said Joel Messcha, extending a business card with his left hand. With his right he grasped Ken's hand as he reached to accept the card. "I'm a real estate sales rep and just happened to be in the area. I've been checking on prices for a client. I know, I know, Messcha is hard to spell and remember. Keep the card, I got plenty."

Joel Messcha looked exactly what a real estate hustler would be expected to look like, from the wingtips on his toes to the implants in his receding scalp. He sweated too much for his light linen jacket and polyester trousers. He sometimes wore and sometimes carried a two hundred and fifty dollar Marc Jacobs white straw hat, the most expensive item in his wardrobe. He wasn't as creepy as Peter Lorre but it seemed he could have stepped out of a 1940s film noir classic.

"You from Pittsburgh?" said Rayna.

"Howd-ja know?"

"*Yinz*. It's a dead giveaway."

"Yep that's the hometown. Used to live right d'ntown in the Triangle, near Market Square."

"Thought so," mumbled Ken, as he began to think about how to get rid of the guy.

Unfortunately the ever-curious Rayna encouraged Joel by asking if he knew of any retirement communities similar to The Villages and still in Central Florida.

Of course Joel's sole job was to hang out around the sales office to cherry pick prospects that might be in the same circumstance as Ken and Rayna.

"I sure do, replied Joel, "what is it you don't like about The Villages?"

"I don't really know," said Rayna. "It's real nice, but it's just too *planned* for my taste. You know, too plastic-fantastic, too neat with golf courses everywhere, planned activities, everyone in those little golf carts. It's like the world of tomorrow inhabited by spooks of the past."

"I know what you mean. If you're a child of the '60s or '70s it's a bit less than the Haight or Woodstock. Not spontaneous enough for ya, I know what you're sayin'. It's all too designed, too scheduled, too white bread."

"Yeh, not exactly, but kinda' like that."

"Got just the place for ya'. I can tell, you're one of those folks who are into nature and like that. You look like a riverfront couple to me."

"I never thought of myself that way," said Ken. "But I think you're right. Waterfront property is awfully expensive though."

"Not when you have an inside track," Joel said in a conspiratorial whisper. "You stick with ole Joel and I can make things happen for you. Things you never imagined. I'm not just some hired hand for the corporation, I know the owners and I can put you in contact with them and some real shakers and breakers, you know what I'm sayin'."

"Well, how much..." Rayna began as Joel broke in.

"No, no, too crass, don't even go there. You *can* afford it. Anyway when you are pursuing you dream and opportunity knocks, don't ask about the price, you start living your dream."

"Yes but..."

"No yes-buts, just go out to property and take a look at Riverfront Dreams—that's the name of the offering," he said, carefully avoiding the terms development or retirement community. "It's a place where dreams can come true for nice folks like you. Hey I think I just made up a slogan, I'm going to keep that one," he said as if he hadn't used the line hundreds and hundreds of times before.

"Thanks a lot anyway," said Ken. "Our car is just over that way and we have reservations for dinner..."

"No, no, no," Joel interrupted. His strong suit was interrupting. "I insist on taking you folks out to one of our finest restaurants for dinner. You do like seafood don't you? If you don't they have a great steak." Always give 'em a question with yes as the only answer. "My Navigator is right this way, we'll take a quick trip out to the property, just for an introductory look around. No tours, nobody's there now. Just a quick look—no pressure—just to give you an idea of what it's all about. Then we have a great dinner and we can talk. Nothing wrong with that is there?" He paused for a beat. "I didn't think so, the Navigator is right over here he said, taking Rayna's arm.

And that's how Ken and Rayna Piccard were introduced to the Florida Real Estate Developer Hustle.

*   *   *   *

In the 1920 to 1930s around the time of the "Great Depression," a rancher was raising what was known as Florida Cracker cattle in an area that would eventually include a housing development known as Riverfront Dreams.

Early in the '20s, long before Florida became "ecologically aware," wetlands were seen as swamps, wasteland to be drained, filled and put into more productive use. No one was aware of the role the wetlands played in the ecosystem that maintained the state's fisheries and agriculture.

Because he needed more grazing land, the unknown rancher filled an area of riverfront that would become the playground of the newly retired. Since the cattle industry had moved further inland, to be later overtaken by The Villages, what was left of the cattle ranch became scrubland once again. In the 1940s it became a fish camp and travel trailer park. In the '80s it became nothing and the remains of the fish camp were removed. An unknown Pittsburgh developer acquired the land in the late '90s and in the early part of the 21st Century, Riverfront Dreams was born.

The part near the river was a high—well, high for Florida—bluff with several acres of filled wetland riverfront below. The lots in the development consisted of riverfront, which was the filled land and as the elevation rose to the roadway behind, river view lots dotted the hillside. Since the river could be seen from the hillside above, every lot that wasn't a riverfront was actually a river view. None were sold as water access because the only lots with access to the river were on the river. Most prospective buyers assumed they would have access to the river and the developers never volunteered information in that regard.

* * * *

Later that evening Ken and Rayna watched the nightly news from their motel bed on a fat screen, CRT television set.

"What do you think," asked Ken.

"About what?" said Rayna innocently?

"The fact this cheap ass motel doesn't have a flat screen TV—don't give me that crap—Riverfront Dreams of course."

"I think Joel Mess-a-wacha is a used car salesman in over his head," she chuckled.

"*I know that*," said Ken emphatically. "What do you think about the property?"

"Isn't Ocklawaha and Indian name for something?"

"I think so, but I'm not sure what. Remind me and I'll look

it up."

"Are you really going back out there with Joel tomorrow? I really didn't have a very good first impression of the place."

"You women are like that; you have to have everything completed and drapes hung, you can't envision how things are going to turn out, you have a limited imagination."

"I'll remember you said that."

"You don't have to go along, you know."

"If I don't go and keep an eye on you two, he'll have you buying the nastiest, swampiest home site in the place and convincing you it's paradise on earth."

*   *   *   *

Joel arrived on the dot the next morning and barged right into the motel room. "You folks ready to begin the dream?" he asked. *Damn, never ask a question they can say no to.*

"We don't want to miss the sun shining through the morning mist rising off the Ocklawaha. You couldn't get the full effect last evening. The live oaks, the Spanish moss, the Sabal palms and the new landscaping. If you squint your eyes, you can imagine Old Florida with steamboats on the river. It's everything you've ever dreamed of in Florida living. It's not that far from The Villages if you want to go there to shop, or a movie, or music on the square. You get a lot of the advantages and none of their costs."

Joel failed to mention that the Ocklawaha has one of Florida's largest populations of very large alligators and he also avoided talk of the constant companions of Florida living, spiders, mosquitoes, and palmetto bugs—a roach by any other name is a roach. Palmetto bugs might be beaten out by Madagascar hissing cockroaches, but not by much. All of the above are real estate hustlers' unmentionables, but all hustlers have a cover story for them. Fortunately, Ken and Rayna were naïve enough not to ask or require an explanation for the unmentionables. Moreover they never asked about the attempts that had been made by the government and growers to screw up the Ocklawaha River or that Ocklawaha is a corruption of an Indian word for muddy. Joel was relieved.

Chapter 7

"Where the hell is Messcha. Ain't he supposed to be on duty at the visitors' center this morning?" asked a semi-perturbed Johnny Stompanato.

"Don't look at me. It was your idea comin' out here today. We didn't come out, we wouldn't even know he wasn't here," offered Louis DeVecchio. "Sides, it wuz your idea to hire him. I know, I know, you wuz suckin' up to that Frank Tropiano guy up in the 'Burg. You owe him or something?"

"Yes, I owe him big time and a lot more people in the business, not just money either. Now get on your cell phone and see if you can raise him."

After several minutes of fumbling with his phone, Louis reported that Joel was out with a couple of live ones and they were looking at that lot down by the river the company was having trouble moving.

"They're down on RF 5, that's the lot where the sewer used to dump in the river. Gotta' get folks down there early before it heats up or it smells like a giant fart," said Louis.

"Have him bring them up here when they finish the tour."

* * * *

"The good luck stars are shining on you guys today. I see the big bosses are on site and will be able to meet with us," said Joel as he opened the office door. "Not everyone gets to meet the big guys. You are really, really lucky."

Ken and Rayna were pushed through the door and directed

to seats in front of Johnny who was sitting behind an ornate walnut desk that was on a platform raised four inches higher than floor level. Louis was sitting in a dark corner just behind Johnny. It seemed he wasn't even there. Joel made the introductions to Johnny ignoring Louis. Ken reached across the desk to shake hands with Johnny.

"Let me introduce you to a major executive in the corporation. My business liaison, Mr. Louis DeVecchio. Louis does all the stuff I can't," explained Johnny. Louis offered a feeble salute of recognition.

Johnny began his spiel, telling them, he knew what they were thinking. "Here's corporate big shot who is only giving us the time of day because we happened along while he's here. Nothing, I repeat nothing could be further from the truth."

"The truth is the very foundation of our values here at Riverfront," said Louis as if he had memorized it by rote—which he had.

"The truth is, I'm not a big shot. We don't have any of those at Riverfront. Here, we all work together with folks like you, helping you find the home place of your dreams. Notice I said home place. You shouldn't feel it's anything other than a place to call home. Tell me a little about yourselves and what brings you to Riverfront Dreams."

Ken wanted to tell him the big stupid guy with the white hat brought him, but he bit his tongue.

"Um, ah, we, Rayna here and… we were looking around at retirement property, went on The Villages tour and met

Mr. DeVecchio and last night; he took us for a quick look and then very kindly treated us to dinner. We're from up in Pennsylvania—on the southern border, um, state line. I taught at a university in Rainelle and recently retired from…"

"I see," Johnny broke in before his head exploded from hearing another retirement story. "Please, please, don't think of Riverfront Dreams as a retirement property. You will find it is a place where you can further your lifestyle expectations and live out your dreams. Have you found anything that interests you yet?"

"I really like RF 5, but Mr. … Joel said he couldn't tell me the price. What's that all about?" said Ken.

"Once you are satisfied with your selection we can talk price Mr. Um Mr.?" Offered Johnny

"Piccard. Well, I'm not sure right now—"

"That's no problem Mr. Piccard, we can settle the matter on the spot. If the owners can't come up with a price, who can?" Johnny said with a chuckle.

"I think they would like RF20 much better than five," suggested Joel with a knowing look toward Johnny.

Louis, who only responded with a big hound-dog look, nodded his head up and down.

"RF20 it is," said Johnny. "How much did you and Mrs. Piccard wish to spend?"

Ken turned to Rayna to ask for her opinion. Rayna looked back, hunched her shoulders and turned her hands palms up. She wasn't getting involved. Ken knew if he made an offer that was ridiculously low the sellers would think they were rubes and if he made one that was too high, he would be screwed.

"I have no idea what it's worth; no idea at all. I couldn't possibly make a serious offer. You let me know your opening price and we'll negotiate from there—too high for my blood, we can part as friends. How does that sound?" Ken said, hopefully.

"We would normally expect to get somewhere around a quarter of a million for a lot that size and remember it's directly on the water, that's what makes it a little pricey," offered Johnny.

"I seen lots that are a little bit bigger go for a million," interrupted Louis who looked as if he'd been napping.

"I'm afraid that would put me in over my head, having to build a house and all."

At this point Johnny and Louis conferred near the back of the room, hopefully out of hearing of either Rayna or Ken. After a few moments, Johnny returned and spoke directly to Ken.

"My associate reminded me of a riverfront lot that already has a display home installed on it that's further up river. It's at the very end of the development, it's out of the way, a bit hard to get to and we could let you have it at a very affordable price."

"What's a very affordable price?" said Ken bluntly.

"We have a luncheon engagement," said Rayna. "We should be getting along. We don't want to take any more of your time, we'll be in touch."

"No need to get in a rush," cautioned Johnny, trying to avoid any appearance of panic. "No reason to miss a once-in-a-lifetime opportunity. Before I scare you off with what may seem to be a high price, let's take a look at it and we'll talk while we look. And, um, your luncheon engagement—if you will just cancel that, Louis, Joel and I will treat you all to lunch."

Johnny, Louis and Joel knew the house they had in mind was no real bargain at any price, it was at the end of a road that rounded a sharp curve and dropped abruptly down to the house and the river below. It was built on a slipping slope of muck fill that had required a heavy application of bribes to get it to pass the inspectors and had been 'sold' numerous times, but the buyers always backed out after they thought it over for a few days. One couple tried to get a legitimate bank loan. The bank's appraiser came out to look the place over, drove down the drive, stepped out of his car, stepped in something brown and gooey, wiped his foot off in the grass, slid back into his sedan and he, the couple and the bank were never heard from again.

Johnny was practically ready to give the thing away just to get the bad luck property out of their hair and get some sales action going.

"Tell you what; I'm going to have Joel run you down there for an in-depth look… examination of the place. And, Mrs. Piccard, please don't make a spur of the moment decision.

You have to envision the dream, think longer term, put your mind's eye to work and imagine how it will look with other houses nearby. Imagine a boat dock, a screened in boathouse where you can party. The house doesn't have a pool, but in a few years you may want one, a barbecue, a patio let yourself imagine, let yourself dream, live your fantasies."

Chapter 8

A little luck, a lowball price, a primed couple, a sales agreement and most importantly, an earnest money check and the deal was on. Ken and Rayna Piccard weren't hooked yet but they were nibbling. Like any deal, all it would take was some more talking, convincing, persuading and making it seem to the couple they were giving the salespersons a king-size screwing.

Financing was the problem most developers had—finding gullible buyers with enough resources to finance the purchase. This was the key to the success of Riverfront Dreams. Where money was counted in terms of suitcases of currency, financing was never a problem. Moreover those who couldn't afford a mortgage on a lot in a fish camp were always able to get a loan at Riverfront at an interesting interest rate.

Joel's favorite close was to play the sucker like a fish. Let them nibble the bait. Taste it, taste it, pull it back.

"I'm not sure about selling it so low. I'll have to confer with the boss."

Let them take the bait in, worry it around a while, make

it seem like the offer was going to be withdrawn, then set the hook. Get a decent amount of up-front earnest money—enough to make them think they weren't able to back out. Then, spring the trap—the closing.

* * * *

"You know, you should have a lawyer to represent you at closing," advised Johnny. "You probably aren't familiar with any good attorneys down here. You don't have a family lawyer who can practice in Florida, do you?"

He watched as Ken and Rayna exchanged looks of the lost.

"Not to worry, we're here to help. No problem, no problem at all." Johnny reached into a vest pocket and withdrew a business card folder and offered Ken a card. "This attorney— Ambrogino Bellucci is very reputable and represents buyers all the time. I think he does it full time. Now don't you go thinking he works for me. He will be representing you; if you hire him, he's *your* lawyer."

* * * *

For Johnny, Louis and Joel things went into high-speed mode at Riverfront Dreams. No waiting on appraisers, no waiting on banks, no waiting for attorneys to draft a deed, just a quick e-mail from Frank Tropiano with only two characters 'OK' and the closing was scheduled.

It was a simple affair held in the same office in which the sale was made. Cheap champagne from a bottle with a towel that covered the label and the toast concluded the proceedings.

The closing was closed.

"Whew?" exclaimed Louis. "I'm always glad when it's over. You never know if they'll suddenly wise up and realize…"

"Hey, Louis, "said Johnny, not this time. They got a great deal. I would almost snap up a deal like that myself. Oh, I'll admit I was a little concerned when they were signing for the homeowners Association covenants, but the thing that Bellucci guy made up looked like it was the real deal. I figure if they ever get around to reading the actual covenants there will be some buyer's remorse. Of course if they bitch, we have their signatures that they received it, that's all we need."

Chapter 9

Moving day came and went without a hitch and Kenneth and Rayna Piccard became firmly ensconced in their new dwelling on the Ocklawaha River.

That evening Ken and Rayna retired to the back deck, or as it was called in Pennsylvania, screen porch. In Riverfront Dreams it's a Florida Room, or for the Florida hoity-toity, a lanai. Glasses of Merlot in hand the couple relaxed on a double recliner.

Through the limbs of a giant cypress off to their left they could see the moon having its reflection broken by the waters of the river. A great white heron swooped, barely above the water on a trip to its nest. Anhingas nesting in a clump of trees to the right chatted their good nights as they settled for the evening while a lone Osprey screamed and dove toward the surface of the Ocklawaha. It plunged downward until its talons found the back of a great fish and then it soared skyward shaking its prey as it zoomed back to a treetop on the other side of the river.

"Ah, this is the good life," murmured Ken as he took

Rayna's hand. "This is the stuff dreams are made of."

"Riverfront dreams," reminded Rayna.

"I think we did good."

Out in the river there appeared to be short flat boards or logs floating here and there. On closer examination, Ken could see two knots on each board that appeared to be set six to ten inches back from the front of it.

On even closer examination Ken came to realize the boards were the heads of several alligators swimming with their bodies just below the surface. Ken had heard the formula for estimating the length of a Florida alligator: The length of the head in inches equals its body length in feet. *Shit, that thing has to be twelve or thirteen feet long.*

He thought better of mentioning the gators to Rayna. He didn't see any reason to hear her complain about being up to their necks in alligators for the rest of the night.

"What the hell is that?" said Rayna.

"What the hell is what?"

"Don't give me that; that thing crawling up our driveway."

* * * *

A greeting committee consisting of some of the other residents stopped by to introduce themselves and drop off some goodies, brochures about Riverfront activities and organizations. The men drifted off to the Florida room and the women congregated in the kitchen/dining room area where they opened the goody basket.

Larry Winters stuck out a hand to Ken. "Larry here, great to have you aboard, so to speak. How do you like Riverfront so far?"

Ken took the hand and shook it ever so briefly. Larry had one of those handshakes that made you feel like scrubbing your hand afterward.

"I'm the President of the Association so I'm guessing you'll get to know all about me from everyone else."

"Association?"

"Oh yeah, you're new. The H.O.A.—the Home Owners Association."

"Let me introduce myself," came a voice from behind Larry.

"I'm Trent Gates." Trent extended a handshake that was the polar opposite of Larry's. "Yep, old Larry here runs one of the most powerful, perhaps, *the* most powerful governing body in America."

Ken immediately sensed an animosity between the two.

"Oh, Trent you know that's an exaggeration. We serve at the will of the residents," said Larry as he took a sip of lemonade, grinning a big ear-to-ear politician's grin.

Trent popped a mini-hotdog in his mouth and began to walk away. "You'll see Kenny my boy, you'll find out."

"Don't mind Trent. He's upset because the board found against him when he submitted a proposal to plant a new tree on his property last week," said Larry.

"You have to have permission to plant a tree?" asked Ken incredulously.

"Oh my yes, if we didn't you might have Brazilian Pepper trees taking over the whole development. We have to look out for invasive exotics that just aren't Riverfront Dreams."

"What did Trent want to plant anyway?" Kent pictured some octopus-looking thing stretching overgrown Kudzu-like tentacles everywhere.

"Come to think of it, I don't remember much about it. It was one of those scrubby looking palm things as I recall— one that no one on the board liked. Have you read your covenants?"

"I looked the booklet over," said Ken, "but I don't recall anything about plants in them."

"Oh, I understand, I know what you're saying. The things the developers get you to sign off on, those aren't the covenants. They are just some summaries they put together for new owners. Tell you what, stop by sometime and I'll give you a complete copy of the covenants. I'm up on Hilly Way, 101 Hilly Way."

"I'll do just that," said Ken emphatically.

"In the meanwhile if you want to do anything, just let me know and I'll tell you if you are in compliance or not."

"What do you mean if I need to do anything?"

"Just like I said, *anything.*"

Ken thought that while he had the ear of the head cheese of the place, he would ask a question so he wouldn't get into any premature trouble with the Association.

"My wife's cousin is thinking about bringing his motor

home down for a tour of Florida. Any problem with him parking in my drive and staying with us for a couple of weeks?"

"'Page 17, paragraph 13, subparagraph 10, line 4. Vehicles not the property of the home owner are not to be parked for longer than a twenty-four hour period.' Even if they stay in the house and leave the camper in storage, they can stay for no longer than two weeks. And if they have kids under twelve, they have to stay elsewhere. They can visit, but not stay."

"What?"

"I know, I know. Lots of regs, but remember, there are many, many advantages to HOA living. Security and knowing someone isn't going to put a junkyard next door and you neighbor isn't one of those hoarders like you see on TV. Believe me, the regulations are for your benefit. It helps keep the riff raff out, if you know what I mean."

And Mussolini made the trains run better, thought Ken. Maybe it was all for the best, but now he was beginning to have doubts about his move to Riverfront Dreams.

* * * *

"How did the kitchen gab-fest go? Learn anything about your new neighbors?" Ken inquired of Rayna.

"Seem like pretty normal folks," offered Rayna.

Ken found this less than comforting knowing that Rayna considered the denizens of faculty wives clubs 'normal.' They went through the entire evening with no mention of 'The Association,' so Ken assumed it wasn't worth mentioning.

Wives tended to talk more about personalities, children, and careers—not politics.

Just as Rayna was ready to switch off the reading lamp at her bedside, she turned and said, "Cousin Eddy and the kids are going to be down next week. They're going to Disney, then stay with us for a few days to see the sights."

Chapter 10

Jayna's cousin cut the family trip short. They stayed a half-day. It was either that or euthanize one of the kids. They took the less drastic route and said a premature good bye.

Ken and Rayna gradually adjusted to retirement life on the river. Ken was embroiled in dispute after dispute with the 'Association' and Rayna learned more and more about the wives and partners of the residents of Riverfront Dreams.

Encouraged by the people he bought the property from; Ken explored the possibility of installing a pool in the back yard. He had plans and a proposal drawn up and submitted them to the board. He didn't go to the meeting, but got the results immediately from Trent Gates.

"Hell, they didn't look at it for more than a few minutes tops. Olga Bachmeier, an ex-kindergarten art teacher, considers herself an expert on aesthetics. She took one look and declared it ugly and from then on the thing was lost. She's the one that torpedoed my tree planting," said Trent.

"Just like that? No expert opinion, no engineers or architects?" said Ken in disbelief.

"What for? They didn't break any laws or violate any statute."

"You think it would do any good for me to re-submit?"

Trent laughed. "Nope!"

"Well, tell me then, what's the appeal process?"

"That's the beauty of it—there is none."

"What about due process? Isn't that a Constitutional Right?"

"Ya' gotta' be kidding me, right? All that stuff has been litigated in the past hundreds of time. If you want to lose some money, hire an attorney and try to fight it."

"That hopeless huh?"

"Right, rights are whatever they decide they are. If you have a problem with a neighbor and he turns you in to the Association for something, it will happen in secret, the board will take it up—serve as judge, jury and executioner. You won't even be able to find out who brought the charges."

Percy Bergeron made no bones about it. He was sure there were racists on the board who had determined to keep blacks at bay in Riverfront. Percy was one fourth African, so he reckoned as how that was what got him through the 'character check.' One of the main obstacles to residency was a little block in the form that asked the prospective homeowner their race.

"Oh, they can't tell you that's how you were excluded; they'll come up with something defensible. I'm white enough to get in, but not enough to run for office or be on a committee," he said. "If anyone had a black wife, they'd never get in, but if it's a black partner, they probably wouldn't mess with you at all. That would be an entirely different kettle of fish."

"You mean they have couples living together that aren't married?" asked Ken, again in disbelief. "I'm sure the covenants say the house must be occupied by a the owner and his spouse."

"First of all, who is going to bring the matter up? Lots of retirees lose their spouse, and then someone moves in for companionship. They don't get married because of financial reasons, loss of alimony payments, pensions, insurance, tax issues, all kinds of reasons. It's kind of overlooked. On the other hand, if they are the same sex, everyone will avoid that issue like the plague. However, if one of them is of a different race—

There may have been racists in Riverfront, but homophobes kept even a lower profile. Of course there were laws preventing discrimination, but then what's a gated community for anyway? Ken learned there were lots of rules and regulations that had to be 'interpreted' by the board.

Larry Winters put it this way, "If everything was engraved in stone and we had to follow the rules, what would we need with a board?"

* * * *

The very next week, Ken's plans for a barbecue were shot down as well. He wanted to have a real wood-fired barbecue grill built of stone. As it turned out the 'Green Committee' took issue with the plan. In the report, the chairman explained the only fuel for outdoor cooking would be electricity only— no wood, even for flavoring and no natural or unnatural gas. As it turned out, the committee didn't have a problem with air pollution, they just preferred any polluting that was necessary was far removed from Riverfront, not in their back yard.

Ken resubmitted his plan to the entire Association board with what was essentially an electric range inside a masonry shell. Olga thought it was ugly and let the committee know it was her 'expert' opinion the barbeque should never be built. "The only place Mr. Piccard can put it is out in front of his home and, as we all are aware, that sort of thing just isn't done in Riverview," she concluded with finality.

The patio went pretty much the same way the pool. Olga thought the stamped concrete paving was gauche. To add insult to injury an 'expert' on civil engineering Klaus Gaertner, who had been a toy designer, convinced the other members of the board that there was no suitable space between the river bank and the rear of the house for anything either.

After having been turned down for his pool and barbecue, Ken decided to go along to the meeting with his designer/ architect to resubmit his plans for the patio to the board. The patio project went the same way as the pool. It was Olga-ed to death.

* * * *

"Are you going to do something about the nasty

overgrowth of weeds in the river off our backyard?" asked Rayna.

Ken thought the water was shallow enough so that he could wade out to where the worst of the weeds were and cut them off with his handy, dandy Weed Zonker—if he kept a close eye out for alligators. He had a brief vision of a legless, former Riverfront Dreams resident selling pencils on a street corner.

He was getting the machine out of his garage and was filling it with gasoline when Larry Winters appeared at the head of the driveway. He trotted down the slope screaming, "whoa."

"What the heck do you think you are doing?" he asked.

"I'm about to cut those nasty weeds back there"

"No you're not, unless you want to pay a hefty fine to the Environmental Protection Agency, another one to the Department of Natural Resources, one to the River Management Agency, another one to the Water Authority and one more to the HOA."

"How am I ever going to build my boat dock and boat house with all those weeds choking things off?"

"You don't have to worry about the weeds."

"I don't? But you just said—

"You don't have to worry about the weeds, they are the least of your problem. If you have enough money for the consultants, the studies and the permits they might even let you cut down a few weeds. But that's not going to do you any good."

"Okay, tell me why that's the rest of my problem."

"The water's too shallow to begin with and you can't afford to dredge it any deeper. All those nasty studies and permits, not to mention the dredging itself. Secondly, what you plan to build would be too close to your house. Can't have the place looking like one of those old fish camps now can we? Olga would have a hissy fit."

From this point on Ken began to keep score on a felt-tip marker board he hung in the game room.

Proposal to remove an old dead cypress tree where he had planned to put the boat dock: denied. An arborist said it was still alive. "It does have cypress leaf beetles, traces of fall webworms, twig gall midge, rust mites and some needle blight. A few hundred dollars should fix it right up," reported the happy arborist.

Proposal to hire an animal control expert to remove a raccoon nest: denied. Animal rights people would raise hell with the Association.

Proposal to plant a palm tree in front of the cypress tree: denied. Olga doesn't like palm trees.

Proposal to erect a barrier to keep alligators out of the back yard: denied. Animal rights people would raise hell with the Association.

Proposal to remove Spanish moss from a live oak in the side yard: denied. Some such tommyrot as "Spanish moss is symbolic of the old south." Olga thought the moss was romantic.

Chapter 11

It was around this time that Ken began to realize he must have pissed off someone who happened to be a board member and he would never be able to accomplish anything.

In desperation he called his attorney Ambrogino Bellucci.

"Who is it?" asked Bellucci.

"It's me. Remember Ken... Kenneth Piccard."

Silence.

"You know the guy you represented in the Riverfront Dreams sale?"

"No."

"Kenneth and Rayna Piccard. We bought the house down on the river, RF30, you surely remember."

"Oh, yeah, now I remember you. Wife was wearin' stretch pants, a blonde, nice bu—. Uh, no offense, I just happened to notice, that's all."

Ken felt his stomach churning.

"I thought maybe you would consider representing me in an action against the homeowners Association," Ken said.

"Not that I don't want to help out understand, but I'm so

bogged down with work, I can't fit any more in right now. There are a bunch of lawyers around this area and I'm sure you'll find someone who'll help."

"Well…"began Ken.

"Click!"

Damn, he hung up on me. That's a fine way for an attorney to act. I guess I'll have to find someone else.

First he searched online where he found several phone numbers and a few e-mail addresses. He tried to limit his search to attorneys who were HOA experts, but found most of them represented HOAs in the region.

One of the so-called experts answered his e-mail query and let him know he represented several HOAs and he didn't believe any of the attorneys involved with associations would want to represent an owner since it might jeopardize their chance to work for any given association at some future date.

This information cut into his list to an astonishing degree so, for the present, he gave up his quest for an attorney. He thought it would be best to ask around and see what some of the neighbors thought about his idea of hiring a lawyer.

* * * *

The community building wasn't much, but it did have a few pool tables, banquet tables and card tables. There was a pool outside and the requisite shuffleboard courts dominated the entranceway. Plain stucco and obligatory Florida coral pink, paint covered the outside. The landscape had been xariscaped with economy in mind; gravel, concrete,

Washingtonian palms, cactus and Spanish bayonet.

Inside the décor look as if it had been lifted from refurbished trailers and the relatively new carpeting was already showing signs of wear. In the middle of the main room several men were playing cards while others watched and kibitzed. Ken joined the watchers.

A few of the watchers introduced themselves and began to tell each other the latest Internet jokes. As it turned out, all of them had shared the same jokes, but they all laughed like they heard them for the first time. A few of the older guys who had Luddite computer knowledge sat out the Internet gabfest.

All politics is local, so the subject of conversation turned to the candidates who were running for the Association board.

"Know anybody running?" asked Nick Naylor a portly gentleman who stood every bit of five feet one inch high. "Lilly Dodd has my vote," he said to no one in particular.

"Why?" said Trent Gates?

"Well, um, I don't know exactly; she seems real nice and she bakes a great lemon meringue pie."

"I'm voting for that sweet thang Mrs. Allwood she's really hot and recently divorced. Maybe give her something she's lacking, if you know what I mean," added Brad Hammar with a leering snigger.

"You dumb asses, that's no reason to vote for someone," chided Dean Brackenridge.

"Who you votin' for Mr. Smarty Drawers?" said a perturbed Nick.

"Someone who has common sense, which may be a hard commodity to find these days. Someone who will consider the facts and not vote for something because of how they feel, what their friends want, or what *they* like."

The conversation went around and around. Most people were casting their votes for an assortment of reasons, none of which made much sense to Ken.

Finally, he broke in, "Hey everybody I need some advice."

An awful silence reigned for about seven seconds. An unseen clock was heard ticking from somewhere in the back of the room and florescent lights that seemed silent until now buzzed away.

"Now you're talking said Dean. We got a whole colon-load of that. Ask away."

Ken nervously cleared his throat. "I think most of you know I've submitted several—eight I think—things to the board. I seems they just turn them down out of hand."

"Yeah?" said about three of the guys who were now listening.

"Well, I was thinking—

"Not a good idea, every time I try it, I wished I hadn't," offered Nick.

"I'm thinking of hiring a lawyer and giving the board and that Larry Winters and his henchwoman Olga a hard time. What they need is a good lawsuit to straighten them out."

There was a muffled gasp, a chortle and the silence returned in earnest.

Trent Gates said, "You're freaking serious aren't you? You ain't messin' with us."

At this point Trent recognized things could get out of hand and jumped in to attempt to set a new tone. "That's a little harsh Nick, I don't think you mean— Ken is new, I think he may be a bit naïve but not... you know..."

By now the card game had come to a halt and everyone was staring at Ken.

"Okay, so someone tell me where I'm going wrong. Someone enlighten me," he said with more bravado than he felt.

"Look," began Trent, "Leon Rutkowski researched this pretty carefully a couple of years back. He had a quarrel with the Association and was thinking about a lawsuit. It never happened but he learned a lot. Why don't you talk it over with Leon before you do anything stupi... um—rash."

* * * *

Weeks passed and Ken forgot about contacting Rutkowski until one night there was a news report of an irate homeowner who became enraged with the president of his homeowner's Association and beat the living crap out of him. "Shing Tseng, an immigrant of Chinese extraction is being held in the Volusia County Jail pending his arraignment on charges of making terroristic threats, battery and assault with intention to do bodily harm," said the announcer.

73

Immediately Ken pulled out his cell phone and called Leon Rutkowski.

"Hello, is this the Rutkowski residence? Is Leon there?"

"I think so, who should I tell him is calling?"

"This is Ken Piccard, I live down on Riverview at the end of Riverview Drive."

"Hold on please, I'll get him."

There was a brief wait, then what sounded like an older man answered. "Hello Ken, this is Leon, what can I do for you?"

"I was shooting the bull with some of the guys up at the community building a few days ago and they said you have had some dealings with the Association and you might be able to give me some advice. You know, your personal experiences."

"Sure, glad to help, but this is going to be between the two of us—right?"

"Absolutely, we can meet at my place or yours. Just the two of us, no one else needs to know about it. It'll be just like that Service Star ad, 'Like it never happened.' My place or yours?"

"Stop by in the evening, say about 6:00-ish. Freda goes to work out about that time, so we'll have the place to ourselves."

"You got a date."

* * * *

Ken arrived at the Rutkowski home at 7:00 sharp. He brought a bottle of wine as a gift hoping it might lubricate

Leon and he would talk more openly. As it turned out the wine wasn't needed. Leon went on and on.

"Let me start," began Leon, "by telling you what you may already know. You are fighting an uphill, if not impossible battle. I'm not saying you are going to lose, but there are far more homeowners who are losers than winners in these fights."

"I'm beginning to get that impression," said Ken with a grimace."

"My experience with the Association: I'll leave out the dates and some of the details. This all happened several months ago. It started with what they called a 'gardening violation.' That's what landed me in hot water," he explained

He planted too many roses on his half-acre property. When the Association fined him, he refused to pay, then sat back while they assessed monthly fines and the bills mounted. After they saw he wouldn't pay, they placed a lien on his property and threatened to foreclose.

"No one knows this of course, that's why we are meeting on the hush-hush. If you tell anyone, I'll deny it. I took the board to court, but lost on the grounds that I had violated the Association's architectural design rules. In addition to planting the roses, I also had the lawn regraded. In the end, I got stuck with the Association's $70,000 legal bills. That's the part I don't want to get out."

"Man that's a serious chunk of change."

"That's what the guys on TV call paying dumb tax. I had enough in my retirement account to pay it off, but they would have put a lien on my place and garnished any income until I paid it anyway. If I hadn't had the money, they would have taken my house, no question."

"Holy moley, that's an expensive lesson. So you're advising me not to get involved in litigation with them?"

"Not necessarily. I'm not big on advice. I'll just tell you about my experiences and you can make up your mind from there.

"Many people who belong to homeowners Associations just don't understand how much power these groups have over them—until they miss a payment or otherwise run afoul of the board. Fall a single day behind in paying your monthly dues, for instance, and the Association may slap you with a fine. Fall 90 days behind and they may place a lien on your home and threaten to foreclose unless you pay up immediately. And because you often hand over the right of property trustee to the Association when you agree to the by-laws, in some cases you don't even get to go to court. That is exactly the case in Riverfront Dreams."

"Riverfront *Dreams*, pretty ironic, huh? More like *nightmare*," commented Ken.

"I've heard that a number of times. It gets worse, there was this one woman, who will remain nameless, had a mistake in the amount of her dues. The board, who often don't know very much about anything and who are trained on the job, made the error, but in the end a judge ruled she was wrong in not paying the amount the board requested while the matter was being disputed. She was left with a $22,000 bill for the Association's legal costs, late fees and interest."

"Now that really sucks," said Ken, "what if she went to the press? You know, get the media involved, rub their noses in it."

"Hey, why didn't I think of that? Think about it for a while."

Several silent moments passed until Ken asked, "So, I thought it over. Tell me where am I going wrong. Why not go to the press?"

"Let's assume they take your side. It's a far reach they would be interested in any homeowners dispute. These disputes are as common as fire ants in a cow pasture."

"I should have guessed."

"Let's assume you have some friends in the media or someone you can bribe to raise a stink. Suppose things are so bad you want to sell out and move. Do you want the world—the market—to know that Riverfront Dreams isn't a dreamy place to live? Do you want everyone out there to know that your house is a 'problem' property? Ever try to get a loan on a property embroiled in litigation?"

"You're just full of good news, aren't you? Next I imagine you're going to tell me the contract I signed with Riverfront is worthless."

"No, I'm not telling you that, but with some exceptions it is. You see they have a contract with *you*. Your contract with them, not so much."

"I could see that one coming."

"The law says a majority of the homeowners in an Association have to approve any change in the bylaws. But boards sidestep this by simply changing their house rules, which are as binding as bylaws but can usually be rewritten without asking all the homeowners. Even if you were to be given the rules today, they're probably already out of date because boards constantly make changes to the rules at whim.

"There are some things the government has stepped in on that help. You can put up a TV antenna; cold comfort now that everyone has cable or a little dish. You can fly the American flag, a nice concession to American Citizens. Even that one ran afoul of an association at one point."

"Flying the American flag? Come on now."

"Yep, turned out the fella's neighbor—who happened to be a board member—thought flag-flying patriotism is an expression of right-wing extremism, jingoism and racism. He won the issue on the fact the guy nailed the mount to his house. Of course the architecture committee got involved, but the Association finally claimed that pounding nails into wood constituted a fire hazard. The guy was forced to mount the flag on a free-standing pole."

"I think I've got the picture," said Ken. "If I sue and lose I get to pay the expenses of the suit. I they win, we all get to pay the expenses of the suit. The board, win or lose, never really loses."

"Now you got it," said Leon, as their little talk ended.

Chapter 12

"How'd it go with Rutkowski?" asked Rayna

"It went. Pretty hopeless I think. About the only way you can make a move against an HOA board is to get everyone in the development behind you and you've seen some of the Neanderthals that inhabit this place. About all they know about anything is what they get from the mainstream media and *The View*. Moreover most of them are keeping a low profile. They don't want to make waves and get identified as a 'troublemaker.'"

"Ready to sell and move out?"

"I'm thinking about it. The only problem is we'd suffer a hell of a loss. We paid a whole bunch of money on closing costs, insurance, character checks, entrance fees; set ups and crap that we will never, ever recover. And, given the economy, no one is lining up with cash to make an offer and getting a mortgage is out of the question."

"I know you, you don't want to give those bastards the satisfaction of knowing they won," declared Rayna.

"Doesn't even enter into it. They won from the get go.

They never lose. The game is rigged; they do whatever they want and usually they get away with it. Maybe not every time, but the losses are minimal at best."

"Then it's settled, put this mess on the market. What's to lose? A few thousand dollars? I can see what this is doing to you. You can sit here and stew, or try to get out and cut our losses. If you want to try and sell, I'm behind you one hundred percent."

Chapter 13

"So why do you want to sell... um... Mr. Piccard is it?" asked Joel.

Ken figured he would begin with trying to sell his property from the people he bought it from so he scheduled a meeting with Joel Messcha. He wasn't really serious about trying to get Riverfront Dreams to buy the property, but he thought it might be a place to start. Joel seemed about as interested as a San Francisco liberal buying land in East LA.

"Ya' know—Mr. um... Piccard is it?" began Joel, "we don't buy back anything and we don't sell for the residents. That wouldn't be legal. We have an agreement with the Association..."

"I figured," said Ken dejectedly. "You know, you should talk to those two bosses of yours about getting rid of that Association thing."

"They—we, got nuthin' to do with it. We had to have one, but it's a freely elected autonomous entity, like other governing bodies in the country... uh, except for one thing."

"Yeah, what's that?"

"They have pretty much unlimited powers. Couldn't get rid of 'em if we wanted to."

"Why don't you warn people when they are looking to buy, then?"

"You look like a smart enough fella' Mr. um… Piccard is it? You're smart enough to figure that one out."

"So what should I do?"

"Now I don't usually give advice in these matters, but if I were going to sell a place out here, I'd look for a real estate agent. I can't advise you, mind you, but if it was me, I'd go somewhere besides the Association's agency—which I assume you don't have much use for anyway."

"Any recommendations?" asked Ken, hopefully.

"Not on your life."

* * * *

Ken went home to his tiny den off the bathroom, sat down at his computer, flexed his fingers and to begin the search for a real estate agent. He leaned back, flexed his fingers again then leaned forward to see what was stuck on the screen. He scraped something off the plastic that covered the surface of his new LCD monitor, and then leaned back once again.

He booted up Internet Explorer, looked over a search site, and then tried Firefox, then Chrome. None satisfied him so he went back to Explorer which was set up to default to Google. He typed "mid-florida real estate" into the search area, clicked on "I'm Feeling Lucky," and surely enough came up with a web site entitled "Mid-Florida Real Estate."

After screwing around with the Internet for an hour, he came up with a few agents, but wasn't satisfied with the results. Next he searched Yellow Book for real estate agents in Ocala, Florida. Literally dozens of names came up listed alphabetically.

Knowing names wasn't very helpful, so as a last hope he decided he would ask around the neighborhood. He concluded that Eugene Fenstermacher would be a good start. *Everyone thinks Fenstermacher is Jewish and a retired accountant—a double whammy*, thought Ken. He reasoned that since Gene had recently moved in, he was probably acquainted with a number of agents in the area, so he decided to give him a call.

"Hello, this is Ken Piccard, is Eugene in?"

"This is Gene, how can I help you?"

"I'm glad you asked. I need your help in finding a real estate agent. I know you've been dealing in the region recently so I was hoping you could offer some advice on who I might get to sell my place."

"I didn't know you intended to pull out Ken. That's a real shame, this place could use a few more people like you, people with good common sense."

"I appreciate that Gene, but I've decided I can't fight city hall any longer and I need to find an agent to sell my place."

"I don't know about recommending anyone, but I can sure give you some names to steer clear of. That Rodney Chambers Agency to begin with—good old Hot Rod," he said, sarcastically. "I don't know whether he has other brokers working with him or not, but they tried to sell me a place north of Wildwood that might have been suitable for a migrant labor camp, but it wasn't for me. I still get calls from them, finally had to tell them to put me on their do-not-call list."

"That's good to know, Gene, these days ya' gotta' be careful out there. Knowing who to avoid is almost as good as who to employ."

"These days or any other days. You need to look out for an outfit called the Gino Bellucci agency; a shyster lawyer and his brothers-in-law run it. In my opinion they may be out on parole, if you know what I mean. They may even be mafia linked.

"There's the woman in downtown Leesburg that I used to find my place here. I don't know if that's much of a recommendation, but it's a start. Pat Brisbay's her name. She has a website, so you can pick up her number from there—or better yet—go to her office on East Dixie and pay her a visit. That's what I'd do if I were you."

Ken had just hung up the phone when Rayna called from the back bedroom.

"Did you have some men come out to survey where you were going to put the boat dock?" she asked.

Chapter 14

Long before homeowners associations, Florida's most notorious and successful pirate was Jose Gaspar, better known as Gasparilla. He was also known as Florida's most bloody buccaneer. He stands out among all the pirates because he had a penchant for burying his ill-gotten gains in Florida soil.

Gaspar left Spain at an early age, sailing to the Gulf Coast of Florida where around Charlotte Harbor he found a home for his pirate empire. He based his operations on what is today known as Gasparilla Island.

It is claimed that he and his brother buried 13 casks and chests of treasure in the vicinity of his headquarters and all around the island.

Gasparilla was living the high life until the 1822 when the American Government sent a Navy squadron to end his infamous career.

The Navy decided to disguise a man-of-war as a merchantman to lure Gasparilla into attacking the fully armed ship. When he finally realized he was trapped he committed suicide. He wrapped a heavy chain around himself, jumped into the water and was soon followed by his doomed ship. It's claimed his last words were something about never being captured alive, but that wasn't the last of the Gasparilla story.

The ship contained $1,000,000 in assorted treasure, and according to legend, is still there today. Charlotte Harbor is an ideal spot to go treasure hunting. Also according to legend, you can pick any island and start digging, because Gasparilla's treasure, buried by Jose himself or one of his hundreds of men, is just about anywhere in the region.

Another of Gasparilla's undiscovered treasures, amounting to several thousand or by now, millions of dollars, was buried on Anastasia Island, south of Matanzas Inlet. The site was recorded as being a three-hour walk south of St. Augustine. Again, the treasure was never recovered.

Orfeo Medina-Gaspar claims to have seen a sheet copper map indicating where the treasure was buried. Or it should be said, where the treasure is no longer buried. It should also be noted that Medina-Gaspar couldn't confirm his relationship to the pirate Gaspar. In fact there isn't much evidence to suggest that Jose "Gasparilla" Gaspar, or whoever he was, ever existed.

The only documented evidence is that a man by the name of Juan Gómez lived in the late 19th and very early 20th centuries used to spin fanciful tales of his days as a pirate and member of Gasparilla's crew. His story appeared in a booklet promoting a hotel and it's the only written account of the whole Gasparilla story. However the story was just romantic enough to give birth to a Gasparilla Festival that continues to be a main attraction in the Tampa Bay area today.

Matanzas Inlet, the site of the buried Gaspar's gold is only about fifteen miles west of the St. Johns River. If someone traveled off the Matanzas River and up Moultrie creek they would be even closer to the St. Johns.

Once in the St. Johns, it's not much of a stretch to believe Orfeo Medina-Gaspar's claim that the Anastasia Island treasure was dug up and hauled by canoe up the St. Johns to the Ocklawaha. It's only about 70 miles to Lake Griffin but no one is quite sure what to believe, certainly not the word of Juan Gómez or Orfeo Medina-Gaspar.

The Medina-Gaspar-Gómez tale was fanciful enough to develop into a rural legend about pirate treasure being left along the banks of the Ocklawaha somewhere between Route 42 and Lake Griffin—near an old fish camp.

As Orfeo tells it, "Two dark-skinned men, either African or Cuban, maybe Puerto Rican, dug up the treasure, transported it by canoe to the St. Johns, then up river to the Ocklawaha where they fell sick with fever. Somewhere near Lake Griffin they decided to put the treasure casks overboard and chain them to a large cypress. Barely able to function, their lightened load enabled them to row the length of Lake Griffin to Leesburg where they landed, never to be heard from again."

Some say the dark men died from the fever, some say they were kidnapped and tortured to death when they wouldn't reveal where the treasure was hidden, still others claim the men returned later, picked up the gold and disappeared. The legend continues with the ghosts of the men returning one day to recover their lost loot.

Chapter 15

Neither Jake Summerfield nor Denny Denhart owned a cell phone so they had to pole and scull their skiff into the marina at Johnson's Fish Camp. There they made a phone call to the Lake County Sheriff's Office.

After a brief talk with Dispatcher Edna Delcambre, Jake finally got Marion County Sheriff Gary Noble on the line.

"You sure it's a skull?" said Noble.

"I'm as sure as I'm standing right here. Human skull too. No doubt about it. Denny—Denny Denhart, that's my buddy. He says it's an old one. It's more brown that white, got some kinda' green stuff like moss growing on it. Must have been out there for quite a while."

"You guys bringing it in? Or, do you want me to send a deputy to pick it up? If it's as old as you say, I suppose there's no rush."

"I think we'd rather someone from the law pick it up. We wrapped it up in a towel, but I'm not thrilled about messing with it anymore."

"Well, both of you wait right there. I'll get someone from

the Lady Lake office out in about an hour. I think you're in Lake County and out of my jurisdiction. If you can, wait there until someone from the Lake County Office gets there to take a statement get some more information, understand?"

"We're making arrangements to have our boat picked up. We may be down on the docks when they get here, but we'll not leave."

*   *   *   *

In less than half an hour Sheriff Don Edwards arrived with a deputy to begin the inquiry. Denny and Jake described where and how they had found the object and there was very little they could add from there on.

"Where is it?" asked the Sheriff.

"It's still in the boat, back under the bow seat wrapped up in an old towel. You have my permission to go aboard and pick it up," Jake said shyly. He had no idea what the protocol was in matters such as this.

The sheriff retrieved the object and laid it out on the dock. Using a ballpoint pen he moved the flap of the towel away from the lump that was in the middle.

"Looks like something you'd see in a museum," observed Denny.

"I can't say for certain without forensics looking at it first, but from what I've seen in the past, this isn't some kind of new crime. Looks to me like an artifact, maybe even Indian… uh… I mean Native American. Could be a hundred years old, maybe older."

Jake, never the most sensitive guy around observed, "Ain't no meat on it at all. Course the gators and crawdads would'a got most of it by now anyway. The gators and turtles probably had a real meal on the rest of it, but it just doesn't look fresh does it?"

The sheriff looked a Jake the way a Jack Russell terrier might, cocked his head and rolled his eyes as if to say, who let you out?

By now a small crowd, including some women and small children had gathered on the dock, so the sheriff took his pen and flipped the towel over the object of their curiosity. Then, wrapping it up, he put it on his clipboard and carried it like some kind of trophy on a tray to his waiting car.

"Let's see, I got your phone numbers where you can be reached. If I need anything else, I'll be in touch," he said over his shoulder as he left.

Chapter 16

Orfeo Medina-Gaspar's son, or whoever he was, was older, but not much wiser. He was still determined to hang on the Gaspar handle long after it served any benefit. His main claim to fame came about when texting teenagers discovered his initials.

Orfeo was never one to bathe or shave often enough for polite company, so he had difficulty fitting it. He was short and was often accused of being a Guatemalan—and accusation that put him in a fighting mood. He made his way on various government subsidies and whatever odd jobs he could pick up and lived in a shack off of a sand road between the river and a housing development. It was remote enough for his lifestyle, but close enough to folks who provided part-time employment.

Women, never approached Orfeo especially in his later years, but even before his beard and hair had turned dirty silver, he was never considered much of a catch. He was a loner, a hermit, what a wig picker would have labeled a misanthropic misogynist. This isn't to say he didn't have a friend.

His very best friend—his only friend—was Fabricio Chávez who Orfeo referred to as Fabio. Of course Fabricio had never heard of his namesake, the sometime actor and model Fabio Lanzoni, so the humor of his friend calling him Fabio was lost on him.

Fabio was a bit younger, a bit cleaner, a bit more closely shaven, had darker hair—greasy of course—and didn't smell quite as bad as his best buddy. Both men wore grungy jeans and the almost obligatory long-sleeve blue work shirts. Perhaps they thought it was the uniform of the Hispanic laborer. The traditional straw peon's hat had given way to the ubiquitous ball cap; both men wore tattered and greasy versions they seldom removed. They might have removed them for bathing, but that act was even more seldom.

Fabio enjoyed Orfeo's friendship because of the stories of Pirates and Jose Gaspar, but he enjoyed Orfeo's periodic purchases of Red Dog and Popov even more. Fabio lived a homeless existence, living under bridges and overpasses. He picked up some cash by panhandling on Route 27 near an intersection at the Walmart. He stayed with Orfeo whenever he could but after a weekend drinking binge they usually argued and Orfeo threw him out—one more time.

"I'm tellin' you I seen it in the Tampa Tribune," said Orfeo"You tellin' me you can read? I can't believe that. You can barely count to ten."

"Reading's got nothing to do with smarts, dummy, that's all about how you wuz taught."

"Oh. Anyways, what did you see in the Tampa newspaper?"

"The guy selling it told me to put it back, so I have to remember what it said; an' you know my memory ain't all that good," said Orfeo. "The headline was 'Skull Found in Ocklawaha.'"

"Go on."

"It went on to say the skull was from the 1800s and the guy who owned the skull—while it was still attached—may have been involved in attempt to move Gasparilla's gold from up near St. Augustine down through the chain of lakes to who-knows-where. They found the skull not far from here."

"So tell me Orfeo, why should Fabricio Chávez give a shit. Oh, I admit it's interesting and all that, but so what?"

"Fabio, this may be the greatest thing that's happened in these parts since, since… I don't know." Suddenly words had failed him.

"You got any beer in the icebox?"

"*Cabeza de mierda*, that's you. Listen my daddy told me tales of Juan Gómez. That's the guy who was a pirate with Gasparilla. He talked of a treasure they buried up at Anastasia Island. He claimed two guys found the treasure and took it across the island to the St. Johns."

Fabio was rummaging in the refrigerator looking for beer. He found a can of Red Dog, popped it open and sat back down.

"Well? Go on, I'm all ears."

"You *have* heard of the St. Johns?"

"Yeah, so?"

"The Ocklawaha out there flows into the St. Johns—up from Anastasia Island."

"Up?"

"Yeah, up! The Ocklawaha flows into the St. Johns and both rivers flow *north*. Not many rivers do—over thirty—but the river out there flows north."

"Must-a been a bitch to paddle upstream all that way," observed Fabio.

"Here's the way I've got it figured. You haven't had too much beer have you? There were, according to what Juan Gómez told my grand daddy, there were two men who found the gold and took it upriver."

Fabio grinned at Orfeo, but the older man knew the beer wasn't the problem. He had only one beer in the fridge. Alcohol didn't change Fabio much; he wasn't the brightest bulb in the string.

"Somewhere just north of where Lake Griffin becomes the Ocklawaha, the two hombres got into a fight, either over how the treasure would be split, or maybe they were just stressed out and pissed off from paddling all that way. I think that's how one guy's skull wound up in the river."

"Maybe they got real hungry on the trip…"

"We have an idea of where to look, let's get that old pirogue we got hid out there in the weeds and mess around where they found the skull. We probably won't find anything, but we could have some fun looking," offered Orfeo.

"Apart from knowing they found the skull south of Route 42, we got no place to even begin to look."

"It costs nothing to look. Besides, it'll be lots of fun. We just follow the river and look for a likely spot."

"Yeah, we just look for a three hundred year old cypress tree and look under it. Only problem is how many cypress trees are out there?"

"Gittin' rich is a matter of luck. You get to a casino; you know the odds are against you. You go into business, you know you probably ain't gonna' get rich—

Chapter 17

His first memories of Florida were seeing palm fronds against an azure blue sky from the backseat of his father's 1937 Chevrolet Sedan as they cruised from Georgia, across the state line to the Land of Flowers. Quinn Kussler still had flashbacks of the then-new aroma of that old car mixed with the scent of orange blossoms.

The pre-Disney family headed for a Florida vacation, something only rich people dreamed of. No one in his elementary school class had ever been to 'The Sunshine State' and perhaps they never would. He was one of the lucky ones.

It really wasn't a vacation; his father was looking for seasonal work in the construction trades. All of the contracts up north, in Pennsylvania, had closed down for the winter and work there would be scarce until spring. The family hoped to find work for his dad and a winter vacation for themselves.

As it turned out, Quinn's father found a job and Quinn found himself enrolled in B.C. Graham School in Tampa. He had hoped he would surely escape school while they were in Florida. However, it did turn out, surprisingly, to be something of a vacation after all. The family went to the beaches and did some salt water fishing on weekends.

Late one Friday, they traveled the lonesome overseas highway to the last outpost of civilization, Key West. There they passed the Naval base where Harry Truman stayed when he visited the tiny island and drove past where 'Papa' Hemmingway lived and even saw one of his cats napping on a sidewalk. This was before Key West had Conch Train tours and rental golf carts so, instead, the family drove through the streets that were fairly free of tourist traffic. It was a time when Key West was somewhat seedy and 'conch houses' were considered more dumps than desirable real estate.

The family actually stopped and entered the Key West Aquarium and visited the docks and turtle pens where sea turtles were actually held until they were marketed or eaten. Mrs. Kussler thought it was something like visiting a stockyard and not exotic or romantic at all.

Quinn had seen enough of the keys and Key West to cause him to decide to return sometime and make his home there. He figured if it was good enough for Harry S. and Hemmingway, it was mighty fine for him.

The Kussler family returned seasonally to Tampa for his father's work and Quinn came to feel he was a real native and not a snowbird. They returned year in and year out until the late '50s when Quinn's father succumbed to a mysterious illness that would have been easily diagnosed today as pancreatic cancer.

The almost eighteen-year-old Quinn Kussler told his mother he intended to stay in Florida if she was going to return north to Pennsylvania. She was disappointed and didn't approve, but recognizing she could no longer tell him what to do, the young Quinn packed his sea bag and headed out. He thumbed south to Key West where he found work at odd jobs. He worked hard, saved his money and one day, he was hired as a deckhand on a fishing charter and his seafaring career, or whatever it was, began.

Of course Quinn heard of Mel Fisher, Mo Molinar and dozens of other treasure hunters in the area. It was a bad experience with some of the lesser-known treasure divers that turned Quinn off on associating with those involved in the treasure scene. They resented the competition and the fact that he easily found stuff on the beach before they did and he had an uncanny ability for turning the stuff into cash.

He kept to himself, saved his meager resources and scoured the coasts for anything that washed ashore. Aside from one gold coin, his 'treasure' consisted of fishing floats; cast aside marine hardware that was attractive to tourists and also stumbled across an occasional rare shell.

Magdalini Manolis owned a souvenir shop that sold the junk he gathered and got prices he never dreamed of, let alone thought of asking. She kept twenty percent and he squirreled away the rest for a down payment on his very own boat. To say Quinn was penurious would be disservice to Fagin or Shylock, who by comparison were spendthrifts.

Quinn ate seafood, mostly conch and occasionally a 'bug'—spiny lobster—but usually settled for more common fare, sheepshead or spadefish. Just about all of the cash he earned was saved toward his dream, a boat of his own.

Maybe it would have been better if Maggie Manolis hadn't told Quinn about the boat that was for sale. The boat wasn't much, but she agreed to finance the balance of his down payment, so the deal was on. He figured Maggie would also make some 'other future demands' but he thought he could take care of that eventuality when the time came. She was thirty years his senior and the prospect didn't seem realistic at the time.

In any event, the deal was made. Maggie would provide financing at free interest—although he anticipated her expectations were more than monetary. And, Quinn would continue to provide her with 'collectables' and whatever cash he could scrape together until the debt was paid.

The boat was a mess. The engine needed a lot of work, but Quinn was mechanically skilled but he had to put some cash up front to buy parts which put him behind in his payments to Maggie. He soon learned he could continue to make payments that weren't cash-based, but the payments took more time than he wished to spend on the task. His mother always told him to enjoy what he couldn't avoid, so he made the best of it and his creditor was pleased beyond her wildest hope.

The hull presented a whole other set of problems. It was a fiberglass affair with an oak keel and some other wood components that had seen a whole lot better days. Lots of epoxy and money—more work with Maggie—applied liberally—fixed it, at least a temporary basis.

By the time he owned the boat and freed himself from Maggie he was a few years older and eons wiser. The boat was too small and he was ready to trade up to a larger vessel, one that he could turn into a dive boat that could be relied on as a real treasure hunter.

However, even with a treasure hunting boat, actual treasure remained elusive. He had his moments when he turned up a gold bar or a handful of coins, but the big find eluded him.

Quinn "Cuss" Kussler had been in Key West for more years than he intended, hoping to get a line on one of the many "treasure loaded" wrecks that are still supposed to be in the region. The longer he stayed in the Keys the stronger was his *belief.* A belief that Mel Fisher had sucked up what leftovers had been left behind. He began to doubt that there would ever be another Atocha, the mother lode of all treasure ships.

He was something of a loaner and did his own research as well as exploratory dives. He wasn't crazy enough to dive alone and enlisted Damian Zanakias of Tarpon Springs to accompany him as a safetyman on his survey dives.

* * * *

Sponges are really animals, their bodies consist of jelly-like mesohyl sandwiched between two thin layers of cells. This layer of jelly is allowed to decompose and smells like rotted fish. The sponge boats and the sponge market in Tarpon

Springs could be detected long before one saw them. After the jelly-like stuff was scraped off, the sponge was washed and trimmed, and then it was taken to market—the sponge auction.

Hardly seen as an animal, sponges do not have nervous, digestive or circulatory systems. Instead, most rely on maintaining a constant water flow through their bodies to obtain food and oxygen and to remove wastes.

The few species of sponge that have entirely soft fibrous skeletons with no hard elements have been used by humans over thousands of years for several purposes, including as padding and as cleaning tools. Dolphins have been observed using sponges as tools while foraging.

* * * *

Adrastos Zanakias came to Tarpon Springs, Florida looking for a new and more affluent life. He knew it wouldn't be easy, but he wasn't the sort to look for a free ride. He arrived on a sponge boat from Key West in 1935 when his new country was in the depths of a depression and Dodecanese Boulevard was bustling—not with tourists—but with the unloading and selling of sponges.

Hard-hat diving, diving with a helmet and suit, was relatively new and the full extent of the dangers were as well, relatively unknown. Although he was a master diver, Adrastos wasn't very well prepared with knowledge of the bends, a helmet squeeze and other dangers awaiting him in the Gulf. He did know that the life of a sponge diver could be very short.

Adrastos endured. He endured the good times when the

sponge harvest was bountiful and the bad times of 1946 when the industry was virtually wiped out by a red tide—a naturally occurring, toxic algal bloom. As with many families that live on the edge, it was shortly after this that his son Zanakias was born. He eked out a living working the tourists and the docks until there was a modest recovery of the sponge market. When sponging came back, Adrastos was too old for his locally made Lerios diving helmet and he gave it to his son, who dabbled in sponge fishing and entertaining tourists with exhibition dives.

Zanakias was a free spirit who couldn't be tied to his helmet's umbilicus for long. He was a hit with the tourists and in particular, with tourists' wives.

Dressed in his suit, awaiting the tender who would place the helmet over his head and screw in his face plate he would deliver his spiel to the gathering in a thick Greek accent. Zanakias actually spoke the perfect English he was taught in public school.

"The first Greek sponge divers appeared in Tarpon Springs around 1905. The divers in Greece were looking for new opportunity and where better to find it than in America," went Zanakias' spiel.

"Until the 1900s sponge fishing—really the collecting of sponges—was done using long-handled, three-pronged hooks. The fishing was done from small skiffs with the fisherman looking for sponges through a bucket with a glass bottom.

"The Greeks who came to these waters brought years of tradition along with them. They brought hard-hat diving and plans for their boats—like this one—based on the Mediterranean boats of their homeland.

"Diving for sponges, it turned out, was much more productive than hooking sponges and eventually a large number of Greeks found their way to Tarpon Springs."

Before his tender screwed in his faceplate, Damian playfully scolded the group. "You ain't been buying any of them synthetic sponges have you? You drive a stake in a diver's heart every time you do that. Besides, nothing beats the feel and quality of the real thing," he said suggestively to the gathered women.

Then with a last wink at one of the pretty faces assembled before him he motioned to his tender who put the faceplate in place and tapped the top of the helmet.

Tarpon Springs became a tourist mecca and the late 1960s when the industry was revived by a renewed interest in natural sponges. However it was meager competition for the Mediterranean market. It did recover a bit after the Aegean Sea was infected with an algal bloom but the once thriving sponge trade was never the same, although some sponge harvesting is done to this day.

Most of old Tarpon Springs is intact and tourists can visit Greek restaurants, shops, diving exhibitions at the old sponge docks. They can see the old sponge market and go on sponge diving excursions. The Lerios diving helmet still survives, but is now more of a symbol of what was 'Old Florida' and the Greek colony of Tarpon Springs, than an essential piece of equipment for the sponge harvest.

For several years Damian lived the fancy—free but sometimes hard life of the docks on Dodecanese Boulevard. It was a life among the tourists and the sponge market, odd jobs at the restaurants, shops—and the bars.

No one is quite sure what happened that night in Amyntas' bar, no one saw the actual fight which took place in a booth at the rear and drifted into the kitchen. There one man found a knife and the other man died from a stab wound. Damian claimed it was self-defense, the man attacked him because he found him with his wife and the only thing he could do was to take the knife from the man and defend himself.

The trial was short and with no witness to tell a different story, Zanakias was sentenced to five years probation. If it had been anyone else, they might have walked, but the judge knew the Zanakias family and Damian's predilections.

He became *persona non grata* along Dodecanese and couldn't find employment among his usual pursuits. Depressed, but knowing he had to leave, he begged a ride on a relative's boat and escaped to what he hoped would be another fancy-free existence in Key West. He was not the first person to try it.

Zack was more of a free spirit of the '70s and looked like a younger Gilbert Roland who had played the archetypical Greek sponge diver in *Beneath The Twelve Mile Reef*. His attraction to tourist's wives, as well as their attraction to him, made him a liability on the Tarpon wharves, so he made his way to Key West where he found employment as a deckhand, charter fishing Lothario— and hang-a-bout for Quinn Kussler.

The dive trips on the Keys were becoming fewer and fewer as were trips to the archives in Europe. Cuss had made a comfortable living but he never made the big hit, the one that would allow him to retire without a care. He never counted on an annuity, Social Security and Medicare to see him through his senior years. Like other seniors who planned their retirement by playing the lotto, Cuss planned for his retirement by dreaming the big dream of Treasure with a capital 'T.'

Zanakias came and went. Sometimes he was paid and other times he went out with Cuss for fun. Cuss got older, but not much wiser and as he approached the magic age of 65. His sun-bleached hair long since more the color of the silver he sought and his skin was now dotted with scars from the dermatologist's scalpel. He knew time was getting short for him to realize his big dream, but the dream never died.

"Did you see the morning paper?" asked Zack.

"No. Did I miss something important? I've been dying to find out which celebrities are gay and who is doing who. Is Oprah going to run for president and beat out what's-his-name."?

"Oh I did notice that one of those big ass women politicians has cellulite. Showed her on the beach in a bikini of all things. You'd think a woman like that would have more sense," said Zack with a grin.

"You must have had some news story in mind. Give."

"Says on page two they found a skull up on the Ocklawaha River, up around The Lazy Gator. You know, that bar you can get to by boat."

"So, some guy went overboard and lost his head."

"It's a real old skull and the word around the campfire is that it belongs to one of the guys who dug up some pirate treasure on Anastasia Island. The belief is he and some other guy was paddling the loot upstream—or is that downstream."

"I heard all about that Anastasia treasure. It's tied to some of that Gasparilla bull shit so that pretty much puts it out of the realm of possibility," said Cuss.

"But…

"Let me guess. The two guys got into a fight and the winner dumped the—I'm guessing—it was gold, right?" Cuss continued as if the question was rhetorical, which it was. "He chained the cask—Gasparilla was big on burying casks—of gold to an old cypress tree, and," he paused for effect, "he left it there and never returned. It's there waiting for some poor dumb ass to stumble over and become an instant millionaire."

"Yeah, something like that, only with not nearly that amount of sarcasm," said the now peeved Zack.

"And, you think we should go and look for it, don't you?"

"Uh… um… why not?"

"First of all, the tale has the smell of bovine excrement all over it—that's bull shit—in case you missed English class in the eighth grade. If old Jose Gaspar wasn't involved I might get a little excited, but everybody knows Gasparilla isn't much more than figment of some promoter's imagination and a festival they have every year in Tampa. Hell, Gasparilla sounds like one of those doily things Latinas wear on their heads."

"That's a *mantilla*, Gringo," Zack said, smugly. When I was a kid, we used to take drives in what was then the outback of Old Tampa. His old tub, or rather the old tub they used for the festival was tied up in the Hillsboro River waiting for next year's event. They used to tow that sucker into the middle of the city and guys dressed up like pirates, boozed and shot cannons and fired pistols into the crowd. I don't know how they managed to keep the pirates from drowning or the citizens from being shot," Zack reminisced.

"You tired of the Keys and Tarpon yet?"

"We could get some metal detecting equipment and whatever else you think we'll need. I'll go along on spec. You don't have to pay me. Even with all the limitations, I have a good feeling about it."

Cuss laid out the problems as he saw them: The whole Gaspar connection. He didn't believe the treasure—if it existed at all—was a Gasparilla find.

The whole story about two men finding the treasure and shipping it up the St. Johns and Ocklawaha smelled funny. Why not take it to the coast which was at least as close as it was to the St. Johns?

Did the two mysterious treasure hunters dump the treasure overboard, or did one survive to take it to God knows where?

No one would take anything but gold and if it was gold,

it was probably in a wooden cask. If they had dumped it overboard, the cask would have rotted away and the river would have taken the gold downstream by now. Or— something that heavy would have sunk, almost to China, in the muck at the bottom of the river.

"Too much going against this one," concluded Kussler.

"Suppose Mel Fisher said that about most of the stuff he went after? Where would he be? Sometimes you have to believe in your gut."

"Number one, I don't give a shit if Jose Gaspar or Johnny Depp buried the gold on Anastasia. I think two, or even more, men found it. I think they were taking it to Tampa; that's where all the pirate activity was going on—on the west coast."

"Hold no now, here's where it gets weirder. I'm as sure that treasure is still in a cask—fresh water preserves wood— and still chained to a cypress tree somewhere down along the Oklawaha. I know it as sure as we are sitting here."

"Okay, Grand Pooh-Bah, psychic wizard man, what makes you so sure?"

Zack returned a sheepish grin, hunched his shoulders, got up and walked to the door. "I don't know how I know—I just know," he admitted.

Chapter 18

"What?" Exclaimed Ken.

"There are two men going down the driveway to where you were planning to put the boat dock," said Rayna.

"You can be sure I didn't have anything to do with it. I gave up on putting a dock anywhere near this property weeks ago."

"Maybe the Association is reconsidering your proposal. Stranger things have happened. Maybe they've heard about you contacting an attorney and are extending an olive branch." Rayna was no Pollyanna by a long shot, but she always looked for the best outcome in any situation.

"Yeah, about the time Saddam Hussein gets a permit to sell snow cones to his neighbors in hell. I suppose I should go out and see what they are up to," he said as he grabbed his Florida Marlins cap and headed toward the door at the back deck.

The stairs from the deck led him across the driveway and down to the river where two men were standing near the tree he thought was dead but an arborist claimed was still alive.

"What's up guys?" Ken offered.

"Oh, do you live here?" said a startled Orfeo Medina-Gaspar.

"You got it. You're standing on my property, you know."

"We just looking for our boat, we don't mean no harm. It got away from us last night down by The Lazy Gator bar. You know where that is?"

"Yes, I know where The Lazy Gator is, what does your boat look like, does it have a name?"

At this point Fabio stepped up, hat in hand. He was intent on playing the role of obsequious peon and he certainly looked the part. It's just a little pirogue *señor*, ain't got no name. We just looking for our little boat."

"Well now, exactly why do you think it might be in my back yard?"

Orfeo stepped in front of Fabio and took over in a less submissive manner. "I didn't realize this was your property sir. The riverbank is clear in this area, so we came from north of here and didn't realize…

"Evidently your boat isn't here. You're free to look around, but I'm thinking you should leave as quickly as possible," said Ken.

He went back up the stairs and into the house. Rayna was at the stove busily making something Ken assumed was for dinner.

"What'd they have to say?" she asked.

"Said their boat got loose and they thought it might have drifted to shore on this side of the river."

"Sounds reasonable, you got any reason to think they're up to something?"

"Not really, but I'm going to call the security guy up at the gate. You never know, if they ripped someone off and we don't report they were around, you know a big deal will be made out of it."

Ken reported a few minutes later that the security guy sounded about as enthusiastic as a gourmet who'd been served a dish of pig's feet. When Ken mentioned they were Latinos the guard sighed and told him they had some trouble in the past. Some of "those people" worked in the development as landscapers and their main job had been to learn the lay of the land. A few nights later they came back and every lawnmower, leaf blower, weed wacker and portable barbecue that wasn't chained down was missing. They came back later and swiped outboards, batteries and fishing gear from the boat docks.

"Even if you have your stuff engraved and have the serial numbers for the cops, you ain't getting it back. It's outta' here and up in Georgia or the Carolinas the same day, the guard reported.

Ken hung up the phone and turned to Rayna. "They seemed awfully interested in that big tree."

"The one next door? It might be valuable, but I seriously doubt if anyone is going to dig it up and haul it out. Thieves like mobile stuff."

* * * *

"You thinking what I'm thinking?" said Orfeo.

"I don't know. You know me, thinking is a *dolor en el cerebro.*"

"I know, thinking makes your brain hurt. Did you ever think that if you tried it more often, you might get used to it? Don't tell me, if you think about that, it gives you a headache. I guess you know you are a big *dolor en el asno*—a big pain in my ass.

"Anyway, I think we are onto something. That Anglo may not know it, but my relatives' treasure is right in his own back yard."

"You think so, Orfeo?"

"I'm not one hundred percent sure, but we're sure as hell gonna' find out."

"How we gonna' do that Orfeo?"

Orfeo, being careful to make sure he kept it simple for his friend laid out his plan to search for the treasure. The idea was to start about a quarter of a mile downstream from the Piccard property. Late at night, borrowing a bigger boat with a heavy duty trolling motor, the two men would silently approach he cypress tree and get out to wade around the knees—the knobby roots—of the tree to see if they could locate the treasure by feel.

*   *   *   *

It took Orfeo and Fabio a couple of weeks to get enough money together for a trip up the river to Ken's place. The money was spent on beer—good stuff—not Red Dog. The change allowed them to buy an anchor, a length of chain and some nylon rope. The idea was to pull in close to shore, anchor the boat, get out and wade around near the old cypress tree to see if they could locate anything.

In the event they located the treasure, one of them would tie ropes around the cask and using a longer length of rope, drag it away under water. With a little luck and if it was dark enough, no one would notice them and of course, no one would know the treasure was gone.

*   *   *   *

There was a bare sliver of moon, enough to cause the fog hanging over the water to have a slight glow. Between the security lights on the riverbank and the moonlit radiance, there was barely enough light to see. Unfortunately it wasn't enough to see everything.

All went according to plan and they arrived at the old cypress at Ken's property. They could barely see the tree and its gnarled roots sticking out of the water. A chorus of frogs croaked and insect tenors accompanied them. All of this added to the night song of the Ocklawaha.

"Pretty spooky shit," said Fabio. "I don't like this one bit."

"Of course you don't. When you know there's going to be some work involved you don't like much of anything. Grab a beer and gulp down some courage. If that treasure's here, we'll have it and be on our way in a short-short."

"You gonna take the gold down to Naida Montero's place?"

"That's what I was thinking. There's a dock out behind her

bar where we can tie up the boat and leave the cask underwater tied to one of the pilings."

"Uh... um."

"You got a problem with that?"

"Uh, no, um, ah, yeah," Fabio said in not much more than a whisper.

"Okay, tell me about it. You're afraid of her aren't you? Tell me now and I'll get someone with cajones, yours must be like little dried up raisins."

"I think she's a *bruja*," said Fabio again in a whisper.

"I think she's a *bruja*—a witch," Orfeo mocked. "Don't worry my little *niña*, I'll watch over you and protect you from the big bad *bruja*."

"*Cójale usted.*"

"That's not nice, what if your mamma heard you say such a thing. Now, get over the side and start feeling around with your feet."

"Bull shit! I'll get my tiny little cajones wet—or snapped off by some big alligator. Not me. Let's see the big macho man get over the side and start shuffling *his* feet around."

"You don't think I've got the nerve? You think I'm chicken?" With that, Orfeo slipped over the gunwale of the boat.

Chapter 19

Quinn "Cuss" Kussler and Damian "Zack" Zanakias argued about the Anastasia Island treasure for days. Every day Zack bugged Cuss about the treasure. He countered his every objection and still argued that he knew the treasure was somewhere south of Route 42 along—he felt—the west bank of the river.

"Come on, we can do it. If nothing else, we take a fishing trip up there and while we are at it, we take along your Fisher Underwater Metal Detector and scan what we see as hot spots. We don't make a move until we get some hits on the UMD. What do you say?"

"You know if we have to investigate the hits, what the water is like up there. It's nasty, filled with particulates, weeds, hyacinths, gators, turtles and big nasty gar," said Cuss.

"The water is shallow and wading will probably get the job done. If we have to go deeper we can use that old hooka rig with the rotting hoses that you never use. One of us keeps a lookout for gators and other river monsters. We've had more trouble from hammerheads than we'll ever see from gators.

Besides you don't look like you're overburdened with activity around here. We could both use a vacation."

For the next few days, Cuss busied himself around the house and went to the docks day after day—doing pretty much nothing. Zack hung around, pouting and bitching about missing the opportunity of a lifetime.

Aside from some lights and other salvage junk that washed up on the beach, Cuss hadn't found anything sellable for days, so finally in disgust he told Zack, "Saddle up, get your gear and some fishing poles together. We are going to fish the Ocklawaha."

"If you're going up there for a bass fishing tournament, you can go without me. I'll stay here and eat smoked mullet."

"The fishing expedition is a cover; I'm taking the Fisher with us. You can run it and I'll pilot the boat—if we can find one."

* * * *

Up I-95 to I-75 was a daylong trip of over 425 miles. By the time they reached their motel in Lady Lake it was late afternoon and too late to find a boat. There was a rib joint on the same side of the highway as their motel, so they walked over and back. By that time it was too late to do anything but hit the sack.

"How long you figure we're going to have to be here?" asked Zack.

"I have no idea; long enough to get disgusted and leave I reckon. Who knows with you as the treasure diviner we may just hit it the first few minutes."

"We'll have to lay some ground work first. I know the river is there for anyone that wants to travel on it, but if we start poking around on private property, we might ask permission first."

"If we tell anyone why we're really here, we'll have lookiloos coming out of our ass, not to mention the press. We ain't out in the middle of the Gulf somewhere you know.

"First thing in the morning we go looking to rent a boat, then we start at Lake Griffin and go up to the Route 42 Bridge, get the lay of the place, then if we have time, maybe look for some hot spots. We run into anything, then and only then we talk to landowners about doing some geodetic, or some such research. Now turn the damned TV off and get some sleep."

"Okay daddy."

"G'nite John Boy."

Chapter 20

Orfeo was standing chest deep in the river as Fabio peered over the side in consternation.

"I got a real bad feeling about all of this," Fabio said.

"You want a bad feeling, you get your ass in this water."

"I mean I got a real bad feeling; I think Naida Montero put a... *maldición*—how you say—*hex* on us. I never liked that old lady. You know, I didn't say anything, but I saw blood on the water on the way over here."

"You always talkin' about seeing blood on the water. You maybe should get your eyes checked. You know, you're making me feel real good, down here in all this muddy crap and telling me about your damned feelings. Shut up and keep an eye out for snakes."

Fabio went to the bow of the boat and scanned the water. "I can't see no snakes, but then I can't see much of anything. It's too dark. You want I should turn on the flashlight?"

"Don't you dare. You'll have that old gringo who lives in that house over there on the bank down on us and then we'll really have some explaining to do. Just shut up and sit down."

Fabio crouched in the bow, not sitting and not standing, but intently trying to see what Orfeo was doing. The water was now almost up to his friend's neck and he was feeling around the bottom with his feet. Or, he *would* have been feeling around the bottom if he could have found it among all of the cypress knees and roots along the bank.

Fabio anxiously asked Orfeo if he could feel anything like a cask. The trouble was neither of them knew what the size of any cask might be. It was assumed it would be about the size of a beer keg people would take to a party.

"*Madre de Dios!*" said Orfeo. It wasn't an exclamation of fear or shock. Given the circumstances of standing almost up to his neck in a river at night, he sounded almost matter of fact.

"What is it *amigo?*"

"I think something just went by my leg, maybe an otter or big fish. Whatever it was, I think it's gone now."

Thank God I'm in the boat. I wouldn't get in that water if all of 'El Dorado' were down there.

Fabio gave out a low moan and whispered a prayer of deliverance from all the *brujas* and Naida Montero in particular.

"Quit mumbling and hold out the oar so I can grab it and move around to the other side of that group of cypress knees," complained Orfeo. "And quit-cher damned pissing and moaning."

Using the extended oar, Orfeo maneuvered in the water and then dragged the boat and Fabio closer in to the big cypress tree.

"I can feel something down there," Orfeo said as he reached down with one hand. There was no way he could reach the bottom without putting his head under the muddy water.

"Don't do it!" Shouted Fabio, "Please, please, oh *Madre de Dios,* please, don't to it!

Once again Fabio gave out a low moan and whispered his prayer for deliverance only this time his prayer was interrupted by a horrendous splashing and a scream from Orfeo.

Unexpectedly, a hand came up out of the water and grabbed Fabio's wrist and before he could brace himself to avoid being pulled in, Fabio was floundering in the water beside Orfeo and whatever had dragged them into the Ocklawaha.

Chapter 21

Foregoing the delights of the Denny's across the street from the motel and unable to separate the taste of Styrofoam from frozen flapjacks, Quinn Kussler and Damian Zanakias eschewed the free continental breakfast in favor of a local mom and pop diner.

"Here's what I have figured; if you have other ideas feel free to jump in," said Cuss.

He outlined his plan of the day to Zanakias. They would drive down to the Dora Canal and from there take a tour boat that would take them through Haynes Creek and down river to Moss Bluff or Route 42 and back to the Lake Eustis side of the Dora Canal. They would be with a group of other tourists and wouldn't attract attention as they took notes and pictures of the tour. It was, according to Cuss, a perfect cover and they could sit back, relax and take it easy for another day. If they found something of interest, they could ask the tour guide to pull in for a closer examination.

The boat was a comfortable three-pontoon affair that was fitted out for a couple of dozen tourists, complete with a fold-down facility for those who imbibed too much beer and a cooler for those with a more persistent thirst.

It was a typical day on the water with lots of bird watching and the spotting a few alligators who cooperated with the photographers who stumbled from one side of the boat to the other to frame a shot of a real, wild Florida gator.

Except for the stuff that excited the wildlife aficionados, the day was fairly uneventful. Zack had dozed off a couple of times and Cuss had to elbow him into semi- consciousness while he busied himself taking notes and a few photographs.

"Whatcha taking pichures of?" asked a curious fellow traveler. "They ain't no birds or animals over there."

"Oh, I'm studying the flora of the region. This particular part of the river has some very rare plant life as well as some invasive species that should be eradicated from Florida waterways. You do know about invasive species, don't you?"

The guy looked down at his camera, fiddled with a dial on top and turned back to center a Great Blue Heron in his viewfinder. This was his way of saying; I ain't talking to no egg heads.

And that was just what Cuss had intended. He continued to make notes and consult his phone/GPS. He carefully recorded the coordinates of every possible spot along the riverbank. Fortunately, in the part of the river that interested him there were few cypress trees. Not that the old cypress of treasure lore was still there, but it was about the only thing he could cling to. Cuss knew that it was very possible this tree could date back to the time pirates roamed the coasts of Florida and it could be even years older than that. It crossed his mind to consult with the dozing psychic, Zack, but decided it would just make for more ill will and he let it go.

Glancing at his notes he saw that he had located about a dozen possibilities with two or three standouts. Of particular interest was a huge old tree that appeared to be in its final days. The top branches were gone and the whole thing had a covering of Spanish moss that made it look like a swamp creature from a 1950s "Crypt Keeper" Comic. Cuss took out a number two pencil and drew a line to it and put a big star at the end of the line. *Shoulda' put an X, X marks the spot.*

The tree was a few feet from the riverbank at the end of a paved driveway. The drive evidently belonged to an overbuilt McMansion that was part of a larger housing development. Try as he might, Cuss couldn't see the property sign from the river, so he made a note to look it up on GoogleMaps later. *I'll bet they have an elaborate website.*

* * * *

"I'm telling you Ken, last night I heard a scream down on the river," complained Rayna Piccard to her husband who wasn't in the least bit interested.

"Then, then there was a lot of splashing and yelling. I know—you didn't hear it; you sleep like a rock. You should see about getting a hearing aid, do you know that?" she continued.

"What do you want me to do about it? I'm not a security

person. If you're so concerned about it, go down and have a look-see for yourself."

"I think you should take a ball bat or golf club and go down and see if you can find anything unusual. Who knows, someone could have been murdered. Who knows, there may be a body floating around in practically our own back yard."

Ken could see he would get no peace until he at least made a show of investigating what Rayna believed was an incident near their home.

"I don't have a ball bat," he declared, "I don't even play ball."

"Hey, Mister Macho, you've sure spent enough on golf clubs to have a set or two around. Grab a nine iron and get-cher ass out there."

"Gators probably cleaned up any bodies left floating around anyway," he mumbled to no one in particular as he headed toward the door, picking up a sand wedge as he went. He walked to the end of the driveway, then down the edge of the water. He looked out across the river, poked around in the weeds around the old cypress tree for a minute or two, then turned around and started up the drive once again.

Somehow he had missed the matted black hair at the end of the driveOnce back in the house, Rayna wanted an immediate report. Ken told her there was nothing to report. He claimed he saw an alligator—one of the biggest he'd ever seen and one of those tour-boats heading north on the opposite side of the river.

"If there were any floaters out there, that gator got 'em, all in one gulp from the look of him," reckoned Ken.

"I still say I heard a commotion out there…"

"If there was, everything is back to normal now," said Ken hoping to put the matter to rest.

Chapter 22

Once back in their Lady Lake motel, Zack sprawled on one of the twin beds, complaining he was pooped out from all of the day's activities. Cuss got out the local phone book and began contacting marinas with boats they could rent by the day. Locating an RV park that rented pontoon boats, he called and reserved a twenty-two footer for one hundred and fifty dollars plus tax and fuel. The dock was located at the southern end of the lake, so they would have to travel all the way to the north end to join the Ocklawaha.

"Get off your dead butt, we've got some shopping to do," said Cuss.

They stopped off at the WalMart in Leesburg and picked up some heavy rope, a plastic five-gallon gas can, a couple of gallons of water, some batteries for the metal detector, some bread and lunch meat and other odds and ends that would meet their needs for the day.

Luckily the outboard on the boat was a four stroke so they didn't have to mix oil in their gasoline so Zack filled the car and gas can from the pump at the WalMart. The marina owner insisted they fill the onboard tank at the marina for a dollar more a gallon than it would have cost elsewhere.

Once on board and a quick run-through of operating instructions by the owner and they got through the process of casting off lines and leaving the dock. Neither the lake or river had much in the way of current nor waves since there was no wind, it was sort of like cruising in a bathtub—smooth as silk.

Cuss announced that he intended to cruise up the eastern side of the lake until they reached the mouth of the river, then stay on that side of the channel until they reached the point where the river narrowed as it passed under the bridge that carried Route 42 over the Ocklawaha. Zack lazily nodded his accord.

"You ain't gonna' find much on the east side," declared Zack.

"You know something I don't?"

"Yeah, I think I do. You just aren't in tune with your surroundings—you got no feeling for the vibes around you. On the other hand, I do. I'm tuned in."

"You ain't been smokin' that shit again, have you?"

"See, there you go. You folks who are flat souled have to have some rational explanation for the stuff you can never seem to get a handle on. You got no feeling for it, so it doesn't exist. You wouldn't know a spiritual experience if it came up and bit you in the ass."

"Tell you what. I'll take the batteries out of the metal detector and pitch 'em overboard. You get out your crystals or whatever you use and guide us right to that fortune you know awaits us."

"No! I ain't got no crystals. What I got is right here," Zack punched his forefinger and middle finger into his temple. "I know you don't believe me and there is no way someone who is tied to the here and now, as tight as you are, will ever get it. You know that we who have these abilities are out here. You know that every hunt for anything worthwhile has someone like me. I'll bet if you ask those guys down on the Keys a lot of them will tell you they rely more on their... their gut, their heart, than they do on all the research and techno-gimmicks."

"Okay, okay, don't go getting all pissy with me. How about we do this, I'll lay this chart out on the table over there and you can do whatever you do—hang a plumb bob over it move a weegie board puck, or whatever it is around on it. Wave your magic wand... on second thought—" Cuss laughed, "don't get that out."

"I'll sit here and do what I do, you lay out the chart. North has to be facing real north—that's on that side of room in case you are really insensitive to this—then I'll come over and put this coin on the hot spot. Only one try, no messing around."

No sooner had Cuss laid out the chart with the north side aligned with true north, Zack walked over and with no incantations or mumbo-jumbo, dropped a dime on the place that Cuss had drawn a line with a star at the end.

"X, or in this case the dime, marks the spot," he proclaimed.

"You just put that where I had put a line with a star at the end of it."

"So? So what if I did? You don't know there is anything there and there, sure as hell is no way for me to know—other than what my head tells me."

"Okay, Okay, so you're a freakin' guru. I was going to look there anyway." *Talk about dropping a dime.*

Cuss wasn't giving in to checking the only old cypress tree on the river. He adamantly stuck to his original plan. They would travel downriver to the bridge and turn back from there. They would investigate every hot spot Cuss had marked on his chart and he granted the concession of paying particular attention to the old cypress that they later found was in the backyard of Kenneth and Rayna Piccard.

* * * *

"Any activity on selling our dream house?" asked Rayna.

"We've had more action at the end of the driveway down there by the river than we'll ever have trying to sell this white elephant. I've been thinking of hiring Olga to stand down there to scare he alligators and alien life forms away."

"Didn't you just love it when she told us we didn't need a pool, we could swim in the river?"

"You don't think the alligators are a real threat, do you?"

"They say if you leave them alone and above all don't feed them…"

"Isn't there a law against that?" interrupted Rayna.

"Yeah, carries a five hundred dollar fine too, but that's not going to stop the terminally stupid. Look around you, you have to know there are at least two or three mentally challenged out there who would feed a gator and think it was cool."

"You really think they are that brain dead? Don't answer that, I see what you're saying."

Ken told his wife not to worry. The run of the mill gator will stretch out in the sun on the river bank to warm his body and may even cruise around as if he is hunting. That said, unless they take a straight line toward you, they are pretty harmless and will usually move away from humans.

"They say you can get an idea of the size of a gator by guessing the distance from between his nostrils to between his eyes. Twelve inches equal a twelve-foot gator. The old guy who hangs out at the cypress tree down there—I've never seen him out of the water—he must be almost fifteen feet long."

"What's the biggest one?" asked Rayna.

"The record alligator for Florida is seventeen feet five inches. Now that was one big guy. The stuffed gator up at Gator Joe's in Ocklawaha is fifteen feet seven inches. I think 'our' gator is somewhere near a record. They can live to be 50 or 60 years old ya' know. I figure he's been around for quite a while. A big guy like that won't roam much, so I figure he's made a home at the base of that old cypress I've been trying to get rid of. I'll bet he has a hole under the bank where he hides out."

Chapter 23

Some time had passed since Ken had approached the Association with any requests, so he had steered clear of their meetings. On a whim, and with nothing better to do, he sat in on the annual re-election of the board. Since there was no regulation forbidding it, the sitting members simply reappointed those members whose terms had expired and 'elected' them by unanimous vote of the board. The new members were, of course, allowed to vote for themselves by secret ballot.

"Is that legal," asked Ken, "looks like a rigged deal to me."

"Doesn't look like anyone is going to object," said Trent Gates.

The business taken up during the meeting involved one of the most contentious issues to come before any homeowners' association—pets.

An anonymous complaint—the use of the word anonymous here is redundant—all complaints were unsigned and anonymous. This allowed board members to file complaints against those who disagreed with them. Anyway, the complaint suggested that a resident owned and kept in his home a dog that was overweight. A rule had been passed that only pets under forty pounds were allowed.

Olga Bachmeier reckoned as how it was her personal opinion that all pets were a nuisance and should be banned.

Fortunately, some of the other board members owned pets and cooler heads prevailed and Olga's pet-ban motion died for lack of a second. However that didn't prevent the board from moving ahead with the "fat dog matter" as the issue came to be known.

"How do we know the dog is overweight?" asked one of the cooler heads.

"Hell, you can look at the damned thing and tell," replied the miffed Olga. This was the first time in which her personal opinion was questioned by the board.

"We've got a package scale in the office, get that fat boy up here and we'll weigh him," said chairman Larry Winters.

"What-cha' mean *we*? Does that mean the royal we, as in *you?*" said Olga.

"We will get one of the maintenance men to do it."

"Never mind the maintenance man, he'll want to be paid overtime, get the damned thing up here and I'll do it myself. If we had any men on this board…

Despite her name, Olga Bachmeier wasn't the least bit Nordic looking. From her name alone, one might have suspected she would be a babushka-wearing, dumpy housewife type. Nothing was further from the truth. This isn't to say she was as attractive as she believed she was by a long shot.

Her typical every-day costume consisted of a close—too close—fitting jump suit with, depending on the day, an animal print. Sometimes she wore leopard spots, sometimes zebra stripes, sometimes tiger markings all adorned pants that were made of some unidentifiable stretch material. White rimmed glasses suspended from time to time with a rhinestone-bedecked leash helped her from drawing attention to her overly done make-up and plucked eyebrows. Ample underarm skin flapped as she gestured, the skin was accompanied by flapping breasts that seemed to be made of the same material. Bright red dyed hair and a butt that looked more like mud flaps rounded out the package that was Olga Bachmeier. She was a sight to behold, except that no one wanted to look.

She was born in West Virginia and considered that to be mark against her in the "High Society" of Riverfront Dreams. Olga harbored deep feelings of inadequacy and resentment. She married, but the relationship was short lived when her husband, Raymond put an end to himself one dark and lonely night while Olga was at the local cinema. She would always claim it was an accident, but an inquest found it was suicide.

Anyone who found out about the closely guarded secret of Raymond's demise assumed, perhaps correctly, that his mistake was his self-inflicted marriage to a woman who would be voted most likely to cause her husband to eat a gun.

She moved on to Ohio where she lived a lonely existence as a public school art teacher and leader of several feminist campaigns that were more intended to promote progressive causes and candidates than they were to ensure equal treatment for women.

Olga's problem was she had no clue as to what she actually looked like. She had a prima-donna air about her and self-confidence that bordered on attitude. In other words she gave new meaning to the term arrogant.

Anyway, the scales and the dog were summoned to the presence of Olga. The poor mutt was a scroungey looking cur that cowered before her. The dog must have known he was doomed before he reluctantly mounted the scales with his tail between his legs.

Olga dragged the poor, scared dog to the platform in what must have been something similar to a prisoner led to a scaffold for execution.

"Forty three pounds pronounced Olga. This bad puppy has to go. Not realizing the stickler for rules that Olga was, one of the clearer heads petitioned for mercy.

"It's only a couple of pounds over, maybe the owner can put him on a diet," he pleaded.

A wag in the back of the room remarked in a stage whisper, "Maybe they could cut off a leg and bring him in compliance.

"The dog's owner Frank Wupperman who was more obsequious than the dog, stepped forward and put a leash on the animal. "I'll take care of him from here. I prefer he isn't exposed to folks like you people any longer than necessary. Yesterday I bought a gold candlestick for Saint Francis, I thought that would help. But I can see all of you—all of you in this… this place are unmoved by human kindness."

All of the residents knew old Frank had a screw loose, or was suffering from the early stages of Alzheimer's disease. In his condition, he wasn't going to be much of a challenge for Olga. He did elicit a modicum of pity from the gathered throng, but nothing that could withstand Olga's determination to have done with the dog and no one would stand up to her.

"Don't worry Ms. Bachmeier, I'll see that Pilar doesn't bother anyone here again."

Chapter 24

Sheriff Don Edwards and his deputy Cheryl Campos walked into Naida Montero's waterfront bar and grill. The sign over the façade announced it was *"NAIDA'S BARRACRUDA"*—Naida's Raw Bar. Of course the locals called it Naida's Barracuda. Naida's was no different than a half-dozen other waterfront dives on the river and the chain of lakes.

It was decked out in fishnets, floats, stuffed Bass and a fiberglass marlin. Old Florida pictures of the place and its denizens adorned rough lumber and rusted tin interior walls and there was a screened-in area overlooking a rickety dock where errant boaters could tie up.

The sheriff and his deputy found seats in a booth across from the bar and waited for a server.

"All out of the special. U-peel shrimp are cheap right now though, got an all-you-can-eat price," said Naida who had never moved from her position behind the bar.

"Hamburger for each of us. Lettuce, tomato, onion and mayo on one, the other one, the same way, only with mustard, no mayo. Make sure they're well done," Don ordered.

"What to drink?"

"Two cokes with two glasses with ice on the side."

"Comin' right up."

Don told Cheryl he was going to the restroom and would return shortly. It was an excuse to check the place out. He wondered around as if looking for the clearly-marked men's room, then made a quick trip to the screened-in area, and finally to the men's room where he washed his hands before returning to the booth.

"You guys are Lake County?" asked Naida.

"Says that on the shoulder patch," offered Cheryl, showing her shoulder insignia.

"Oh, I see. I'm not used to having the law in here, at least as customers."

"Well, today we aren't just customers. I'd like to ask you some questions if you don't mind."

"No *problema*. Ask away."

The sheriff explained they were looking for Orfeo and Fabricio who were last seen in a small boat on the Ocklawaha.

"Names aren't familiar," she said. "That doesn't mean they haven't been in here. Lots of guys come in regular, but they aren't very open with their names. I usually give them a nickname so I can kinda remember them. What they do?

"We don't know that they did anything," said Don casually as he flipped the lettuce off of his hamburger.

"Whatcha do that for?" asked his deputy. "If you didn't

want lettuce why ask for it?"

"They always put it on no matter what I order. It's easier to throw it away than try to get them to leave it off."

"Why the ice on the side? I usually order it with Coke poured over the ice."

"Yeah, you usually get about a table spoon of Coke and a glassful of ice water too."

"If they didn't do nothin' why you lookin' for them?" said Naida.

"A guy they borrowed a boat off of reported them missing when his boat wasn't returned. Later, the boat turned up, but the two men never did."

"Probably sleeping it off somewhere," opined Naida.

"Could be, but I have a feeling something bad happened to them. There's a lot of water out there and a lot of toothy things looking for a meal."

"You think one of them might have killed the other and is hiding out?"

"Doubtful, but you never know," the sheriff said. "How about a check and we'll get out of here?"

* * * *

Sheriff Edwards and deputy Cheryl Campos were coming up on the place where Jake Summerfield and Denny Denhart had found the skull a few weeks back. Cheryl had the misfortune of making sure the thing made it back to the crime lab.

Now they were on another 'fun' cruise, searching the river

for the remains of a couple of ne'er-do-well Latinos, who had been missing for, well, no one knew for how long. They were *reported* missing about a week ago. Long enough to assume they hadn't just up and gone off to parts unknown. The one most concerned was the owner of a boat they had borrowed. The boat turned up without the men about the time of the missing persons' report.

"Most likely got drunk and fell overboard," opined Don.

"Maybe got into a fight and both went for an unintended swim," replied Cheryl. "I doubt if they ever turn up, lots and lots of gators out here."

"Yeah, get ten or twelve of those toothy critters together and a Hispanic or two ain't gonna be much of a meal. Gone in a few gulps. They usually take a body somewhere to rot for a while before they feed, so there wouldn't be much left to find unless we were… uh… let me rephrase that, unlucky. Unlucky enough to find any leftovers."

"Did you notice the two guys in the pontoon boat when we passed the inlet to Haines Creek? They appeared to be looking for something. You don't suppose they're looking for the same things we are? You think we should go back and pull alongside and ask some questions?" asked Cheryl.

"Naw, no point in taking up any more time with this than we have to. We probably wouldn't turn up anything we don't already know. I think we'll skip it."

As they approached the site of where the skull was found, Don switched off the big outboards and dropped the trolling motor. The intent was to cruise the riverbank in hopes of finding at least something. After a quarter-mile of this he went back to the outboards. At a point about one thousand yards north of the big cypress at Riverfront Dreams, he switched back to the troller.

"*Hey*," shouted Cheryl, "there is something over there." She motioned, waving Don over toward the cypress. "There, down among the knees on the right, looks like hair—black hair."

Don expertly guided the boat through the shallow water and gnarled knees until they were about ten feet from a patch of black hair that ebbed and flowed like eel grass in the current they had stirred up.

"You got that boat hook back there somewhere?" asked Cheryl.

Don picked up a collapsible boat hook and handed it to her. She extended the thing to its full length and asked her pilot to get even closer.

"I don't want to run aground if I can help it," he said as he eased the trolling motor throttle forward. "You can never tell what you are liable to hit."

"That's it, if you can hold it right there, I think we're close enough."

The Deputy reached out and eased the hook end into the mat of hair. "Well, I don't think it's Hispanic."

"What makes you so sure?"

"It ain't a Chihuahua, too big. It's a damned dog. What do

you want me to do now?"

"See if you can ease it out our way. We'll drag it up on the bank and pick it up later. There's a driveway coming down from that housing development and we'll bring the pickup down, take a closer look and then dispose of it properly," said the conscientious Sheriff.

"Why you suppose the gators didn't gobble it up?"

"Gotta' get ripe first."

"Ew."

＊　＊　＊　＊

Ken and Rayna had gone shopping at the WalMart in The Villages so no one was around when a lone figure ventured down their driveway and into their back yard. Perhaps his intent was to stroll the riverbank just for the exercise, but when he spotted a fairly large lump of black hair his interest was aroused.

The man left immediately, returned with a piece of plastic sheeting, hurriedly wrapped the object in it and carried it away.

Chapter 25

By now Ken had developed a practice of going to Association meetings primarily for the entertainment value. This particular meeting had a different ambiance however. A sort of pall hung over the gathering and Ken had arrived too late to separate out someone to ask what was up.

After the pledge to the flag and the reading of the minutes Larry Winters asked for a moment of silence for the 'beloved' member of the board Olga Bachmeier who had suffered some sort of 'spell' and was hospitalized.

Mumbling came from the back row of seats. "Heart attack... stroke... aneurism. Too bad... yeah, *right*."

Larry asked one of his friends on the board to introduce a motion honoring Ms. Bachmeier but one of those with a clearer head objected to such a motion. He claimed it was premature and would set a precedent of passing a resolution to honor a living board member.

"Maybe if we wait a while, she can become eligible," mumbled someone from the direction of Trent Gates. Trent later denied saying it.

There was no further information provided, so Ken hung around after the meeting in the hope of picking up some gossip tidbits.

"Okay," Ken said to Trent, "what gives with Olga?"

"Beats the heck out of me. Someone—and believe me, I don't have a clue who it was—hung a dead dog on her deck. Took down a hanging basket of flowers and replaced it with the dog, hanged him on the hook by his collar. And no, it's not *the* dog you're thinking about—the one she was determined be removed from the development. It looks nothing at all like it, except it's black. About the right size, a little bigger though."

"If you *did* have a clue, you wouldn't say a word about it would you Trent?"

"Yeah, but suppose—suppose she meets the qualifications for honorable mention by the Association?"

"It would be a shame, I guess, but I wouldn't shed any tears. Not many people I can say that about," commented Ken, "but in her case, I might make an exception. She was—ah, *is*-" he corrected himself, "a real pain the posterior."

"I'm glad I didn't see it. I'll bet she not only had chest pains, but crapped her leotards when she saw that thing hanging there."

"If she passes on—dies—whatever, it could go hard on the person or persons that did it. That is if they ever catch them. I think you can see, the less said about this he better."

"Where'd the dog come from?" asked Ken.

"Sheriff's deputy came out from Lady Lake and picked it

up. He said the sheriff and a female deputy found it in the river and towed it over to that old cypress behind your place and left it to be picked up later. Heck, that was right in your own back yard."

"Any idea about a prognosis?"

"Bitch like that ain't gonna just up and die. Jim Morrison aside, it's too late for her to live fast, die young and leave a good looking corpse. Only the good die young and if she went tonight, she had it on a downhill drag.

"No, I expect she'll survive. Her kind always do, Trent added."

"You know," began Ken, "I really feel sorry for old man Wupperman. Having all this stress in his life after his wife died and everything. I get the feeling he's just hanging out waiting for God to call."

"Don't spend too much pity capital on Frank. You can say that about everyone who lives here. In a way, we are all hanging out in the waiting room awaiting the call."

"Yeah, I know, I know, but I like to think—to fantasize. Maybe I'll do something to make a difference, someday it may all amount to something… someday."

Chapter 26

Don Edwards, the Sheriff of Lake County, appeared at Ken's door. He inquired if Ken or his wife knew anything about a dog that was in his backyard—he gestured toward the cypress tree on the riverbank.

Ken admitted he hadn't actually seen the dog, but had heard that it was involved in an incident in the development.

"Yes," said Don, "the ah… the—," he fumbled with his notes. "—The Bachmeier lady, someone said they found it hanging on her porch. She saw it and freaked out, poor woman."

"Poor woman," repeated Ken, softly.

"I suppose you don't have any idea who might be involved."

It may have been a foul mood, or just a feeling he had to somehow get even, so he went ahead anyway.

"As a matter of fact I do. I have a comprehensive list." He turned and picked up the Riverfront Dreams phone and address book. "Here ya' go, if you eliminate her friends who were members of the board and Landro Marino you will have a complete list of anyone who might have wanted to mess with her."

"What's with Landro Marino, why eliminate him?"

"He died last week, but if he were living…

"I see what you're saying. Olga was not a person who was—shall we say—universally loved."

"You might say that and, by the way, you probably can't eliminate her 'friends on the board,' they're a couple of two-faced bastards. Don't get me wrong; I don't think anyone would want to kill her. I think they all would like to see her—as one of the board attendees put it, "crap her leotards."

"And, who might that have been?"

"I have no idea. I was sitting near the front of the room when it was being discussed. It was just one of those comments people make, sort of off-the-cuff."

"Did anyone attempt to identify or claim the dog?"

"It wasn't from around here, no tags on the collar. No one seems to know where the thing came from."

The Sheriff told Ken that he didn't think there was much he could do to further investigate the matter at this point and unless Olga took a turn for the worse, it wasn't any more than a tasteless prank and he couldn't see spending any more of the county's money on a prank.

* * * *

It took three more days for Olga to qualify for Official HOA Honors. The coroner's report concluded an aneurism caused by shock was the cause of death.

The sheriff's threat to open an investigation if Olga died was pretty toothless because he and everyone else knew that even if malicious intent was proven, it would be difficult to get much of a conviction for a death that couldn't have been foreseen. All of that aside, there was no evidence except for the pickled body of a dog in the forensics lab that was awaiting the incinerator.

There was a ceremony that was attended by Olga's board-member friends and a cousin who was imported from Michigan. The fest… ah solemn ceremony included placing a gold star—that was really bronze— beside Olga's name on the roll of past board members.

Oh, Frank Wupperman also attended. After the ceremony he held court at the shuffleboard area outside the meeting room. Those in attendance were Brownie, a fox terrier, Ricky a Chihuahua, Bubba a Yorkie and unidentified cat. The only other attendee was a 'homeless' man who happened to wander by.

"Perhaps no one will remember this day. Maybe no one will remember Olga Bachmeier and it's just possible that's the way it should be for folks like her. Some of us just sit in the waiting room and await our turn to try the pearly gates. Olga's heart wasn't made that way. While she waited, something happened to her heart and it ossified. Sorry Bubba, that means it turned to stone. Bubba looked up at Frank, cocked his head and whimpered.

Chapter 27

Don Edwards and his deputy Cheryl Campos used the hanging dog incident to its fullest. They had escaped at least two days of looking for the missing Latinos who had lost a boat on the river. Since there was no family to protest the suspension of the search, Don and Cheryl simply gave up the hunt and filed the final missing persons' paperwork on them. "The owner of the boat got his boat back, the county got all their papers signed and Don believed that eventually a shack that was inhabited by a *vejete*, an old geezer who would never be missed, would be taken over by the state. So it was for the riverfront dreams of El Dorado.

* * * *

Damian Zanakias and Quinn Kussler were hosing down the deck of Cuss's old salvage boat because Cuss was thinking of selling it. He hadn't placed any advertisements on the thing, but he had a small for sale sign tacked to the railing. It was a feeble attempt that matched his unwillingness to let go of past dreams of treasure.

"Hey Cuss, ya think the law down on the Ocklawaha has

cleared out of there yet?"

"Maybe, why?"

"I told you, we left too early. I think if we had stuck around a while longer we might have found that cask we were looking for."

"Look pal, that's a 425 mile trip. Almost 1,000 miles roundtrip, you want to pay for the gas, I'll kick in the wear, tear, oil money, but that's it."

"Does that mean there's a new split on the loot if we find it?"

"No, that means if we come up empty-like with most of your get-rich-quick schemes—I don't get stuck with all the costs."

"You figure $75 will cover the gas?"

"From what I spent the last time, that covers getting there. I'll need another $75 to get back."

"Not to worry about money for getting back. We'll be able to afford new wheels and all the gas we need."

Cuss told Zack he'd think about it, which for anyone else would have meant, end of discussion. However, Zack wasn't wired that way. Zack was a nudge. Cuss didn't know much Yiddish, but he sure knew what a nudge was. Zack was like a dog with a bone. He'd gnaw on Cuss until he finally agreed to make the return trip north; it was only a matter of time.

Cuss reached up and tore the sign off of the handrail and tossed it into the Gulf.

"Okay, okay, enough already. Let me make some calls to

make sure the sheriff is out of the way. If he is, we'll go up this weekend. We shouldn't have to be gone for more than a couple of days. You say you know—you can feel it in your... whatever—where the cask is, so we shouldn't have to waste any time. Just go over there, pick it up, load it in the truck and head home."

"You got it bwana," said Zack. "Minimal sweat, maximum benefit."

"Just one more thing."

"What one more thing?"

"We come up empty, it's all yours and I want an additional $75 for putting up with your miserable ass."

Chapter 28

It was all Cuss's idea if anyone were to ask. On his own, he decided to take a direct approach with the owner of the house behind the big cypress. He knocked on the front door.

"Hello, my name is Donald Miller and I represent Middle Florida Tree Experts. I'd like to speak with the property owner about that big cypress tree behind your place," Cuss said.

"I'm the property owner," said Ken. "What's up?"

"We were in the neighborhood and noticed the condition of the big cypress back there and thought you might be interested in an evaluation of it."

"What do you mean, *evaluation?*"

"It looks like it needs to be taken down and I know how difficult homeowners' associations can be in these matters. We can take a look at it and as certified arborists we can help you make the case with your association."

Hope sprang in Ken's heart. With Olga gone and a certified arborist's report, he might finally be rid of the tree.

"How much is it going to cost me?"

"No charge for the evaluation. If we take the tree down,

we get paid. If not, we make recommendations and you decide what you want to do and how much you want to spend. I don't think you can pass up a deal like that."

Excited by the prospect of ridding his property of the old tree and maybe the alligator he believed lived under it, he quickly asked for an agreement to sign so the work could begin.

"Tell ya' what," said Cuss, "Since we aren't talking money yet, all we need is a handshake and I can get to work."

"You sure you're a certified arborist and have insurance—and everything?"

Cuss pointed to his pickup that he had the foresight to have magnetic signs displayed on the door. "You think I'd go to all the trouble of stealing a company truck so I could go around and assess trees for free?"

Afraid of losing the opportunity of a lifetime, Ken agreed. "I suppose it's all legit. After all, what's to lose?"

"Yeah, what's to lose? I'll get started right away. I have to go pick up my assistant and we'll get on it this afternoon. You can go shopping or whatever you wish. We prefer that the homeowner stays away while we work. Safety and insurance reasons, you know. I'll leave a copy of the report in the door and mail another just in case. Okay?"

At first Ken thought about protesting not being able to observer the workers, but then thought, *what the hell, it's free. I'm never going to hire these guys no matter what the report says.*

*   *   *   *

Orfeo Medina-Gaspar wasn't quite sure how he happened to wake up in one of Fabricio Chávez's *debajo del puente*— under the bridge hideaways. Later, when his head had a chance to clear, he remembered crawling up the driveway beside the big house on the river. That happened after—oh it was too terrible to think about. After Fabio had been taken under the water by something. It must have been the *cocodrilo*—the alligator—that at first grabbed him, then went for Fabio.

Orfeo remembered 'coming alive'—he regained consciousness after being knocked out for a time. He couldn't remember for how long. He could recall flailing the water and working his way to riverbank below the driveway and passing out once more.

It was still dark when he came around and he awoke with a terrible pain in his leg. In the dim light he looked at the wound and discovered he had been bitten by something. It was enough to cause bleeding, but not enough to be a real problem. The alligator, or whatever it was had held him for a while and for some reason had let him go in favor of Fabio. Fabio was nowhere to be seen. If the gator had been human it wouldn't have been a far stretch to imagine he let go of Orfeo because he had a taste preference. Maybe Orfeo had been saved because of his bathing—or lack of—bathing habits.

*   *   *   *

With great difficulty, the small man made his way to Naida Montero's waterfront bar and grill where he sought the pity and assistance of Naida, the *bruja*.

It turned out that Naida was more saint than sinner. If she had been sensible, she would have sent Orfeo packing, but she wasn't sensible and took him in, helped him dress his wound and even helped wash him. It was the first real bath he had in months.

She gave him a pair of old dungarees that were much too big and zipped up the side. The shirt wasn't much better. It buttoned on the 'wrong' side and Orfeo felt it was a challenge to fasten it properly. He had no new underwear, but that didn't matter because he never wore underwear. All in all the diminutive Orfeo believed he was the luckiest man in the world and Naida was his *Madre Teresa*. He felt honor-bound to somehow repay her for her kindness.

"Did you know they are looking for you out on the river? They are also looking for your friend, uh, Fab... Fabricio. They stopped here and asked if we had seen either of you," said Naida.

"*Policía?*"

"Sheriff, I think. You know how the Anglos are. They have a law officer for every nook and cranny. Police, Sheriff, State Police, Agents—it's all the same. They find you, they put your *pequeño asno* in jail and if you're illegal it could be worse."

"*Madre de Dios.*"

"You betcha. Tell me something Orfeo—that's what the sheriff said your name was—what happened to your friend Fabricio. Don't tell me you killed him."

"Oh no, no, no, never. He was my *mejor amigo, numero uno*."

"So, what happened to your number one, best friend? And don't lie to me you little geezer. If I find out you're lying I'll drop a dime on you as sure as you are sitting there."

Orfeo was beginning to reevaluate the *Madre Teresa* thing, as his mind returned to *bruja*.

"Thank you for your kindness, you are a saint to take care of an old man the way you have," he groveled. "Let me stay another day until I'm well enough to move and I'll go back to my home. Just one more day *por favor*? I promise to repay you."

"Yeah, just like all the other freeloaders I get in here. You can stay until morning, then *vamanos*, you got it *vejete?*"

"Well?" asked Naida.

"Well what?"

"Don't play that crap with me, what happened to Fabricio?"

"Honest to God, I don't know. At least I don't know for sure. We were wading in the water…"

"Don't hand me that. You were wading in the Ocklawaha River in the middle of the night?"

"*Si*, Fabricio—not the brightest of men—dropped the anchor overboard and it got caught on some roots," Orfeo lied. "We had to get in the water to get it loose."

"And?"

"First, I felt something grab my leg. I kicked at it with my free foot and it let go, but then it went for Fabio—uh, that's what I call him. Anyway, after what I think was a giant gator got a-hold of him, it dragged him under and that was the last I saw of him. The last thing I remember until I woke up on the river bank."

"Sounds like a whole pants-load to me. Now go and get in the storage room or I'll...."

"Oh *gracias, señora buena hermosa* you are so kind to let me stay."

"And you can forget that kind and beautiful lady shit. I ain't been no lady since... since I became a *vieja arrugada bruja!*"

If Orfeo had a hat, it would have been in both hands, peon-style, as he backed into the storage area, closing the door behind him.

Except for the part about losing the anchor, everything Orfeo had told Naida was the absolute truth—as he knew it.

* * * *

The next day, Orfeo Medina-Gaspar was shaking the cobwebs from his head in one of Fabricio Chávez's *debajo del puente*—under the bridge hideaways—that he had located. His leg was sore and festering a little. Orfeo knew he would have to steal a bottle of the foaming water at one of the convenience stores that lined Route 441/27. He normally avoided stealing, not so much because of his moral upbringing but he knew shoplifting might draw attention to him. So, while he was in the store he got a cardboard box and along with a brown bottle of hydrogen peroxide, he also lifted a used black marker.

Using the marker, he made a 'WILL WORK FOR FOOD SIGN.' Of course he had no intention of working and the sign was simply an attention getter for the bleeding hearts who would pull over to his corner on Route 441 and hand him a few bills—for food of course.

Within a half-hour he was being bugged by one of the regulars who considered the corner his own turf and his property. However, by that time, Orfeo had collected $47.50, much of it in quarters. Now he was enabled to buy a six-pack of Red Dog some jerky and a couple of cans of bean soup. And he had a whole bunch of money left over. He would be able to hide out until the *policia* gave up looking for Fabio.

As it turned out, he didn't have to wait long. Within the next couple of weeks the activity on the river was down to one or two fishing boats every hour or so.

Chapter 29

Zack and Cuss had just left the truck, which they parked, halfway down Ken Piccard's drive. They grabbed a couple of lengths of rope, a long pole and a harness and proceeded to walk toward the big cypress tree.

"At least we won't have to rent a pontoon again. That gets expensive," said Zack.

"Not so fast. If that cask is down there hung up on a root or something, just how do you think we can go about hauling it out without every blue-hair in this place coming down to stick their noses into it?"

"Never thought of that, Cuss. I'm glad you're the brains of this outfit."

"Yeah, I should get a bigger share for the intellect I bring to this operation."

"Hey, man, I'm the soul of this job. Without my mojo where would you be?"

"Probably taking it easy in the Conch Republic," chided Cuss. "Before we start dividing up the loot, what say we find it first?"

"Should I remind you, we've already found it!"

"I think I should remind you—assuming it's there—we still have to locate the cask, pry it out of all that muck, roots and God knows what else, and then by whatever means necessary, secretly haul it to some place where we can examine it in private. Then, and only then, after I see it and hold it, I'll admit you are some sort of psychic genius."

"Hey Cuss, what if the thing is too big or heavy to get up into the truck?"

"I don't think I want to take it out that way anyway. Too great a chance of being spotted. I'm going to tell the homeowner we need to bring in our boat and make a closer examination from the river. First I'll tell him it will cost more and when he gets all ticked off about the cost, I'll tell him it's free and he'll be as happy as a clam."

"Good, I'm content to let you go ahead and be the big brain negotiator, I'll just hang back and play dumb."

"Don't try at playing too hard."

"I knew that was coming, you just gotta' get your digs in, don't you."

By this time the two men were at the water's edge and were peering at the tree's foundation. Cuss held the pole out to Zack and asked him to poke around among the knees and roots to see if he could find anything. By this time, both men were knee deep in the Ocklawaha.

"See if you can get up under the bank a little. If there are any turtles or gators, maybe they'll come…"

At that very instant a huge crocodilian head surfaced and with very little disturbance to the surface, swam off upstream and away from the riverbank.

"Did you see that?" said Zack.

"How could I miss it? That sucker must be eighteen feet long if he's an inch. Let's make sure he's well out of here before we mess around in his bedroom too much."

"You still interested in going after the gold?"

"More than ever. If that big guy has been guarding it for the last half century, it has to still be there."

"Ah... Cuss—I have a weird feeling about this thing. I know, I know, I said I had a feeling about it before, but now it's out of hand. You don't suppose Old Gasparilla put a curse or a hex on this place do you?"

"Look, my superstitious friend, Old Jose Gaspar is more likely a figment of someone's imagination. That aside, he was long gone before the treasure was moved to this site."

"Oh, I never thought of that."

"Unless..."

"Unless what?"

"Ooooo... unless his ghost is still around and he and the *cocodrilo* are keeping watch over his gold," teased Cuss.

"Now, you think you're messing with me, don't you? Messin' with my mind. I'm here to tell you that you may be onto something, something you shouldn't be kidding around about; I take that kind of thing seriously."

"Yeah all you Greeks and your Epiphany Celebration. You

think that you can dive into that freezing ass Spring Bayou and bring up a cross and you'll have good luck for the rest of the year."

"Hey Cuss, now you makin' me mad. That's my Religion you're knocking now. You got to apply to the Church and go through an indoctrination just to participate in that celebration."

"I bet your luck bringing up that cross was about the same as our luck bringing up that cask. You never came close to winning did you?"

"I never got the chance to make the dive," said Zack.

"Only thing most of those guys get is a shrunken nut sack and a load of bad luck. I'm just saying—no disrespect to your religion—your luck for the year or any year is what you make it. Some mystical B.S. isn't going to help. And, you can apply that label to your ghost as well."

"I didn't say I believe in no ghost!" Zack protested, but now you got me wondering. Maybe Gasparilla's ghost is living in that big gator I just ran out of there."

"I'll bet you piped smoke into that diving helmet you wore for the tourists down in Tarpon. I didn't know I was going to be working with some superstitious, ghost fearing, highboots, goatbanger."

"Now you've gone too far. I'm not saying another word. Let's see if we can find that cask and work on getting out of this swamp."

Cuss looked around anxiously, "You haven't seen any sign

of that big gator have you?"

When he got no response, Cuss told Zack he would hang back and await the homeowner's return and ask him to report an unfriendly gator in the river.

"After I get done telling him how we were attacked and how dangerous the gator is—how it's endangering the whole community, the animal control people will be out here to either remove it or kill it."

"They'll do that?"

Cuss explained that Florida has a Statewide Nuisance Alligator Program that's supposed to reduce the threat from bad-boy alligators to people and their property in developed areas. They contract private alligator trappers to remove specific nuisance alligators.

"I believe we can meet the requirements. The property owner has to consent and I'll talk him into filing a nuisance alligator report and for him to get his neighbors to file their own. The only other qualification is the gator has to be over four feet long and I think your "ghost" can meet that requirement and then some."

"You think we can get someone out here all that soon?"

"I'll make a big fuss about how big and dangerous he is and we were attacked and we need to get to work. They'll probably get on it right away. I think Old Ken the property owner will be more than anxious to move things along. You go on back to the motel and wait. I'll be along after I see Ken."

"I'm wet up to my knees."

"Don't worry, you'll dry by the time you get back."

* * * *

Kenneth Piccard arrived late in the afternoon to find who he believed to be Donald Miller the arborist sitting in the back of his pickup truck. Rayna Piccard busied herself taking groceries and other purchases into the house.

"How'd it go?" said Ken.

"Well, you're not gonna' like it. We hit a snag."

Ken's heart sank, "What kind of snag?"

"We waded into the river a few steps to take a closer look at the base of the tree and—see—there's a big alligator living up under that tree somewhere."

"I had a feeling that's where he lived."

"Anyway, he went into full attack mode, headed straight for my assistant. Lucky for him he had a pole and fended him off."

"He didn't get hurt did he?" asked a now concerned Ken.

"He sort of twisted his ankle when he got out of the way, but he's okay, nothing to worry about. It scared the living daylights out of both of us. We're used to seeing all sorts of thing on this job, but that's one big gator."

"What do you think I should do?"

"We sure as heck can't finish this job with him hanging around. Anyone been missing any pets around here?"

"There was a dead… no, no missing pets."

"What you should do is file a nuisance gator report on him. You can get the forms and find out the procedures on the Internet if you have a computer and access. Get some neighbors to sign reports as well. You'll get quicker action that way. They won't act on a little alligator, but you can take my word for it, this guy is over 16 feet long if he's an inch. Try to get someone out here right away. Make an issue of how scared everyone is and dangerous he is. Tell them he attacked two workmen you employed and they have to get a job done for you. We can't hang around this job forever you know."

"I'll get on it right now," said Ken.

"And, tell them he's in an area that isn't natural for an alligator. Tell 'em he's practically living in your driveway."

Spurred on by the prospect of losing a free statement that could end the life of the tree, Ken immediately went to the house to call the Florida Wildlife Commission and to file a report.

Nearly half an hour later, Ken came out to find Cuss still sitting where he left him.

"What did you find out?" Cuss asked.

"Said they'd be out first thing in the morning. I must have said all the right things—or maybe they have a contractor that's anxious to make a buck. Their website said they needed contractors in some of the counties. You ever think about a sideline?"

"No thanks, that's the kind of job where I like to be well out of the way. I've got some experience with sharks, but absolutely none with alligators. It would be something to see those guys pull that big fella out of there, but I'd just as soon be right up here well away from the action."

* * * *

Albert Boudreaux and Leroy Jacques, both natives of Houma, Louisiana, established a lucrative business trapping nuisance animals in the central region of Florida. When the Association called, the trappers submitted the lowest bid to capture the nuisance gator at Riverfront Dreams. Ken would pay half the fee and the Association agreed to fund the other half. Normally the homeowners group wouldn't have gotten involved, but in this case they felt they would score big on public relations and the savings on their insurance policy would more than offset the cost.

Zack and Cuss were caught in a dilemma because of the time element. Their limited resources wouldn't allow them to stay for long and arranging the removal of the gator was taking too long. They decided to move out of their Lady Lake motel and they made arrangements with a fish camp owner on the river to rent one of his empty trailers on a monthly basis. Even if they only stayed for a week or two, they would save big time over motel rates. Of course they had to trade comfort for necessity.

* * * *

Days passed, but finally Albert and Leroy showed up at Ken Piccard's driveway one sunny Saturday afternoon. They backed their pickup down the driveway and maneuvered it as close to the old cypress as possible. While Leroy readied the equipment, Albert surveyed the scene. The plan was to set and fasten firmly, a heavy bamboo pole at the base of the tree and hang a line from it. From the line a huge hook would hold a piece of gamey chicken intended to tempt the gator. The thing would be rigged about two feet off the surface, so that smaller gators wouldn't try for the bait.

Once hooked, the gator wranglers would attempt to haul the gator out of the river and onto the bank. If it wasn't the monster everyone claimed it was, they would tape the beast's mouth shut and wrestle him into the truck. The jaws are a minor concern. After the mouth is taped, a gator's only real weapons are his claws and tail. Those are not minor weapons and one swipe of a lightning fast tail can break legs or kill a man.

"Hey, Leroy, lookee over here," said Albert.

"What-cha got?" replied Leroy.

"See him? His nose be right over there. I think we can get a noose over it and drag him right out of here. This gonna' be easy. Look to me like that sucker is at least a eleven footer."

"Easy part be gettin' the noose on him. Gettin' him in the truck gonna' be hard. Now get that long handled noose, tha' one made outta' aircraft cable. Get the .22, just in case. Don't want to kill 'em, but I ain't getting in his way to do me some damage either," said Leroy.

Albert got the noose and went to the water's edge and began working the noose carefully over the big gator's nose. Just as the noose was in place, he quickly tightened the cable causing the gator to shake his head from side to side as he tried to shake the snare, exploding the water around him.

At the same time Leroy noticed some turbulence and movement among the cypress knees. A second gator was present, one that must be at least eighteen feet long or six feet longer—judging from the length of his head—than the one Albert had—or perhaps it would be better to say, it had Albert.

"Look out there Albert, there's another one over here. He be a lot bigger than the one in the noose. He get pissed, he gonna' be comin' your way. Maybe you best let go and we get the hell outta' here."

Albert was in no mind to let his catch escape. He hung on for dear life and yelled for Leroy to get the rifle.

"You need help out dere?"

"NO," Albert screamed, get the gun NOW!"

Chapter 30

Orfeo Medina-Gaspar had been lying low for days, expecting a visit from the Lake County sheriff at any minute. Little did he know the search for him had been given up right after he and Fabricio Chávez went missing. Still, he only sneaked out of his under-bridge hideout for an hour or so a day. He wore clothing he had purchased from a mission store with handout money and tried to dress like an Anglo. He lifted a pair of shades from the CVS store near Spanish Springs, since he believed the law was looking for a Latino He tried to appear as Anglo as possible, which frankly, wasn't possible.

Once he stopped by to thank Naida Montero for her kindness. He soon learned she was having none of him. "Look-it here geezer, I don't want you coming around here no more, you got that? You got bad luck written all over you," she told him in no uncertain terms as she slammed the door in his face.

Orfeo looked at his arms, but quickly understood Naida's remark about luck was metaphorical and there no bad luck writing that could be seen on him. Nonetheless, he knew it was there and he knew bad luck was dogging him since his experience with the gator under the big cypress tree. If he had known about Zack Zanakias' theory that the gator was harboring the ghost of Jose Gaspar, he would have, no doubt, subscribed to that idea as well. Ghost or not, the creature had been a heap of bad luck for his buddy Fabio.

Orfeo Medina-Gaspar wasn't born in Cuba. His father and mother came from Cuba to work in the Ybor City's cigar factories long before *El Barbudo* took over the tiny island nation and turned it into a 'worker's paradise.' Orfeo became a citizen of the United States by right of birth and he had the papers to prove it. His parents were legally naturalized in the late 1920s so they never lived under the threat of deportation.

Orfeo Medina, senior later became Orfeo Medina-Gaspar on a whim after he had heard a story about the fabled pirate. Although not well educated, he could read. He worked in the Questa-Vina Cigar Factory with the hope of being elected reader. One day the usual "Lector" fell ill and Orfeo agreed to fill in for him.

The tradition of "Lector" was imported to Key West then Tampa and other points where small cigar factories were established. Orfeo's job was to read the daily newspaper to the workman as they sat at their benches making cigars by hand. He also read books, the classics and political treatises of the day. From a platform above the floor, Orfeo held a position high above the rest of the workers and was held in esteem that was commensurate with his physical location. He was a star. In a voice as sure as any Barrymore he read in, crisp

Castilian Spanish. For many workers, this was their only taste of education and none would dare interrupt their teacher, "*EL Lector*", "the Reader."

It was a time when unions were making themselves known and the owners of the factories began to pay a lot more attention to what the readers were reading. New ideas of communism, socialism, and anarchism were being introduced in America and the owners feared the cigar workers would be radicalized by the "Lectors" and organized by the union organizers.

By 1932, Orfeo had to step down from his lofty perch and find more common work at a much lower wage, on the factory floor. The owners found that a new invention—the radio—did almost as well as the readers. The readers and their lofty platforms were torn down and the mellifluous Castilian tones were replace by the blaring electro-magnetic speakers we have all come to know and the title and status of "*El Lector*" was sent to the dustbin of history.

Orfeo Medina-Gaspar, senior was never the same after losing his position as *El Lector*. Of course, he missed the salary, but most of all he missed his former status as the factory star. He missed knowing that his fellows in the factory elected him as a sign of utmost respect. His sense of self-worth suffered perhaps more than his salary.

After working years at the factory, little Orfeo came along. His mother had worked as a housemaid, but with the added duties of Orfeo, she had to quit to take care of the new member

of the family and times were hard. Little Orfeo's father
considered giving up the name Gaspar, but decided it was at
least something that his son might find pride in.

He was sent off to a grammar school where Spanish was
spoken and taught, but English was required. After graduating
from the eighth grade, he worked for a short time at the
Questa-Vina Cigar Factory, but even that job disappeared
as the now well-known process of unionization and
mechanization took its toll on the industry—and labor.

After young Orfeo lost hope of a job, he became the
stereotypical rebellious youth. In the '50s he considered
joining some of the older rambunctious guys in an adventure
that would leave the older boys to an early end in *La Batalla
de Girón.* Luckily Orfeo didn't join them in their *aventura
patriótica magnífica* and didn't depend on the *Norte
Americanos* to pull him out of harm's way. *El Barbudo* took
over Cuba and Orfeo learned lessons of who you can trust
and developed a doubting attitude concerning *gringos.* The
infamous Bay of Pigs wasn't infamous for nothing.

Dogged by the feeling that he and Fabio had discovered the
site of a Gasparilla treasure, he made himself a nest, or a blind,
not far from the old cypress tree so that he could keep an eye
on the increased activity there.

He had seen the two *gringos* messing around the base of
the tree and correctly assumed they were looking for *his* gold.
He assured himself it would have been shared with his friend
Fabio, but since the gator… well, now the treasure was all his

and the two guys fishing around the cypress knees had no right to it. He knew they were going to try to steal it from him.

He knew he had to devise a plan to rescue the
gold if the two Anglos were to claim it for themselves
and take it from the river to who-knows-where.

As the days passed, Orfeo became bolder and he gradually moved out into the open. He grew a Poncho Villa mustache, dyed his hair a dark black and pulled a rakish cowboy hat over his long hair. He looked in the mirror and determined he was no longer identifiable as Orfeo Medina-Gaspar. He looked much younger and since he had lost a few pounds on a meager diet of beans and rice, he believed he was a different person entirely.

He odd-jobbed and panhandled enough money to afford new clothing and a used 9mm Glock. Orfeo had no idea how to use it or why he might need one. He did know that on the street, it was considered a firearm of distinction and a gun that his new persona required. Carrying it gave him a feeling of power, a feeling that no one could dismiss him anymore. Like a true gangsta, he quickly pulled the pistol from his belt and aimed at the man in the mirror—a new version of Orfeo Medina-Gaspar. Another quick glance at the man in the mirror assured him that the old Orfeo—the *vejete* who was looked down on by everyone—including that *repugnante bruja* Naida, was gone. The new Orfeo would show them all, especially Naida who he was thinking might be a little less nasty, given a proper chance and a little money. With the gold from the old cypress tree, he could fulfill his dream, he would have respect, he would *be* the *Nuevo* Orfeo. He would be redeemed and regain the family respect he knew his father had had in *la Florida vieja,* Old Florida.

Orfeo Gasparilla! He would rescue what he now believed to be his inheritance from the hated Anglos who would deprive him of it. He would give handouts to the poor Latinos and become their hero, their *defensor—Nuevo Gasparilla.*

Orfeo decided he would live and sleep in his hideout nest, keeping an eye on the gold that he knew was under the big cypress tree.

* * * *

"What the heck is going on in the backyard?" asked Rayna.

"They are trying to remove that big gator we've been seeing," replied Ken.

"I hope this isn't another of your big messes. I hope those guys have worker's comp or liability or some kind of insurance. If that gator turns around and kills one of those guys, our asses will be in a sling."

"I told you, they are contractors recommended by the state. We are sharing costs with the Association and any liability should be on the State if anything unforeseen happens. The State requires they are insured. It's not supposed to cost more than a few hundred at most."

"Yeah, I've heard all that crap before… several times."

"Why don't you just relax and go take a nap."

"What and miss all the fun? Mix us a couple of Bloody Marys and we'll go out on the deck and watch."

* * * *

Damian Zanakias and Quinn Kussler were sitting in the 'Mid Florida Tree Experts' pickup that was parked on the access road leading to the Piccard residence. They watched intently until the two gator catchers had put a noose around the gator when they heard one of them shout for the other to get the gun.

At that point, Cuss started the truck and at the earliest opportunity, he slipped it into reverse and backed out and turned onto the highway.

"We don't want to be anywhere near here when they pull that big gator out. Anything goes bad, we'll be fat dumb and happy," said Cuss.

"I'm willing to learn all about it from that guy, Ken," said Zack"

They returned to their fish camp dwelling and napped the rest of the afternoon.

Chapter 31

Leroy Jacques came running down the Piccard driveway carrying Albert's Colt M4 Carbine.22 Tactical Rimfire rifle. Albert had bought it because it looked like a military full auto, it looked like a badass gun, but it took cheap .22 caliber ammunition, so he could load it up and shoot it all day for peanuts. It wasn't fully automatic, like a machine gun, but its semi-auto function allowed him to fire every time the trigger was pulled—a definite advantage for gator hunters.

Albert took the rifle from Leroy and without looking to see if there were cartridges in the clip, he jacked one into the chamber. With not much lost motion, he fired four quick rounds somewhere in the vicinity of the alligator's head.

If they had been real gator hunters, Albert wouldn't have been so sloppy with his shooting. Fewer bullet holes make for more expensive hides. However, the hide wasn't a consideration; the main idea was to have a dead gator as quickly as possible. To be sure, Albert fired six more rounds directly into the gator's head as Leroy was beginning to drag the huge carcass ashore.

Albert ran up the drive to the truck and made sure it was in position for loading. He took a cable attached to a winch he called the "Critter Gitter" and handed it to Leroy who slipped the noose off beast's nose and looped the cable around its head.

"What about the oth…" began Leroy.

"AAH," uttered Albert loudly. "We didn't see no other gator."

"But…"

"We didn't see no other gator, *understand?*"

"I guess so."

They winched the gator to the tailgate and both of them, with a great deal of difficulty and help from the winch, lifted the beast into the truck and curled the long tail around so that it fit into the eight-foot bed.

Albert looked up to the deck on the back of the house when he heard someone shout. "Nice work fellas. I'll be right down."

"You need to sign this here paper," Albert said as he handed a form to Ken.

"No problem, I'm really glad to be rid of that thing. What will you do with him now?" asked Ken.

"We got a guy that processes them for us, he helps us cover expenses and we even make a little profit on the deal."

"Well, you guys did a mighty fine job. Glad it wasn't me doing it. It looked pretty dicey there for a while."

"Yeah, you don't have to worry about this gator bothering you no more. That be gar-on-teed," he said in an exaggerated Cajun accent. You got another problem, you just give Ole Albear a call and we be right out, you hear?" Albert said as he handed him one of their business cards.

He turned to Leroy and in a loud whisper beyond Ken's hearing said, "Let's get the hell out of here before dat big sucker come back."

*   *   *   *

Out on the Ocklawaha a Great Blue Heron swooped low over the calm, murky, evening waters, an Osprey screamed and plunged to the surface and rose again, his talons firmly grasping a great fish. To the north, the head of a giant alligator broke the surface as he made a great loop and headed south to his post under the old cypress tree—now that the smaller interloper was gone.

*   *   *   *

Orfeo, who hadn't left his nest all afternoon, noticed the return of the alligator. He admired the animal's great strength and ease with which it swam. *Surely it is the incarnation of Jose Gaspar. Gasparilla still stands guard over the treasure, the treasure that is rightfully mine.*

He also noticed the finality with which the rifle had dispatched the powerful guardian of the Ocklawaha.

Orfeo thought to himself, *it will be interesting to see if those treasure hunting gringos have any better luck with that big old lizard than Fabio and I had.*

Chapter 32

Cuss was having a beer while watching "Sea Hunt" on television and complaining it was dubbed in Spanish, which caused him to drift off into an illegal immigration rant. "You think we should go back out there and resume our 'tree inspection' tomorrow?"

"Oh no, I love lying around in this paradise and listening to you bitch about the world going to hell in a hand-basket," complained Zack.

"I figured you were ready to back out by now. You know a curse on the whole project, no gold, just alligators up to your ass, all that stuff. *Maldición*, ain't that what the Latinos call it?"

"There you go, making fun of what you don't understand. There ain't nothing as ignorant as a person who thinks they know something and they don't know shit."

"Oh, I beg your pardon, oh great *hechicero*, the sorcerer, tha', the *psíquico*."

"Piss what? If you're determined to piss me off that's what you're doing."

"Psíquico, you dumb ass. Psychic!"

"Maybe so, maybe so, "said Zack as if he drifted off into some sort of trance. "I can see it now, down there grown between the knees. It's wood, good stout oak preserved by the freshwater. No wood-eating organisms in fresh water. I figure it's the size of one of those small party kegs, or one of those old nail kegs you seen in antique stores. Something that size would be about the right size for one or two men to handle."

"How you figure we're gonna' get it out from the cypress knees? It's gotta' be in there tight after all these years. Why don't you tune in the infinite and answer me that one."

Zack pondered the problem for a moment. "It would be easy if we didn't have to sneak it out. We'd just get some big equip…"

"I know it would be easy if we had a backhoe and a bulldozer dumb ass. Don't tell me what I already know," Cuss interrupted.

"Don't get your panties all in a knot. All we have to do is get us a come-along—"

"You mean one of those hand-winch things. That's gonna' do nothing but tear the cask apart." Cuss interrupted again.

"You always jump to conclusions. We find the knees and roots holding it and use the come-along to pull them out of the way, leaving that old cask free for the taking. Put some straps around it, and tow it to somewhere where we can load it into the pickup. Cover that thing up with a tarp and head south. We can get a come-along at Lowes and take it back for a refund when we're done."

"Hmmm," mused Cuss, who was beginning to see some merit in Zack's plan.

"What-cha think?"

"If that cask is the size you think it is and if it's filled with gold coins, we'll have to bust our hump. A lotta' work getting a thing like that to where we can get it out of the river. I think we could tow it underwater for a ways, then get it on a dolly and somehow manage to get it into the pickup. I don't think we can roll it around like they did back when it was new. A lot of back breaking work involved fer sure."

"Gold's selling for almost $1,400 an ounce today. You ain't gonna' make that much in the rest of your life. A few hours of muckin' about in the Ocklawaha is nothing compared to the payoff," said Zack

"There's 12 ounces in a pound—that's a troy ounce. I figger there's gotta' be 150 pounds… say… gonna' be what? Over two-and-half million dollars in that cask. And, that's a very conservative estimate and doesn't even consider the fact the gold is in rare, collectable coins. Hell if we have to invest a half-million in the project we can walk away with a lot more than a million apiece."

"That's the first time I ever heard you talk anything like a fifty-fifty split. I think I'm falling in love."

* * * *

Ken Piccard was hoping against hope that the tree experts would return quickly and give him a report that would allow him to petition the Association to cut down the old cypress tree. He was standing in the driveway, looking toward the river, lost in thought concerning the tree when an official looking car pulled into the drive.

"Are you Mr. Piccard, the owner of this property?" asked the driver of the car through a rolled-down window.

"That's me," he said. "Something I can do for you?"

"Depends, I'm one of those inspectors you keep hearing about. Just wanted to check in with you to see if you've noticed any settlement or other geological problem with your house."

"No, why? Is something up?"

"Not really, we work for some attorneys in the area, we're just checking. Just in case, ya' know. You know there are some properties in Florida that are troubled with sinkholes. Not so much a problem here, but more over towards the east. Here, we're on the lookout for subsidence from poor fill or undercutting from water seepage, that sort of thing."

"Uh… no, nothing I know of—"

"No foundation cracks, anything like that?"

"No, but I'll keep an eye out now that you mention it."

Ken hadn't even thought to consider settling or water seepage problems—he had been so focused on the old cypress tree.

Problems, problems, I should have known better than to get involved in all this home owner stuff at my age, thought Ken as he returned to the house.

He immediately went to the utility/laundry room, which

was as close to most Florida houses come to an 'up-north' basement. He never entered the room that contained a washer/dryer because he considered it the domain of Rayna. His preliminary inspection revealed a water stain that extended out from under the washer. *Probably a leak in the washer pump, he said to himself,* hopefully.

Further examination revealed a large crack along the front wall of the entire house and a lateral crack along the entire slab on which the house was sitting. His heart sank. He knew from talking with other homeowners this was a major, major problem. It might involve replacing the whole structure. It would depend on how much the fill under the house was moving.

He spent the entire sleepless night and never thought of the cypress tree once. He was totally focused on a much larger problem. If he contacted a contractor or engineer, it would be evidence he knew about the problem and any subsequent litigation to a buyer would be fraught with economic peril. Of course selling the place didn't seem much of an option at this point either. The real estate market was dead.

If he put off selling, the whole thing might slide into the river, or a void from seeping water might open up and literally swallow the place. He was between a rock and a hard place. The only option was to sell and get out, but nobody was buying. What to do, he'd wait until morning and ask Rayna—she might have some ideas.

When the morning finally came, it turned out that Rayna

had no idea about where to go from here. After about twenty minutes of "told-ja so" followed by what a dumbass he was getting involved in the venture in the first place, she finished with, "You know I never was for it in the first place. That guy with the white hat and the car salesman shoes talked you into it. I went along because I thought it was what you wanted.

"Why don't cha' ask your buddy, Trent Gates what he thinks. He seems to be the one handing out advice around here."

With that Ken stormed out. The only dumb ass thing he done so far was asking Rayna what she felt.

I'm going to do just that Miss Fancy britches—bitch.

* * * *

"If you're busy I can come back some other time," Ken said as Trent came to the door wiping his hands on a dinner napkin.

"Oh no, I was just finishing dinner. The wife's away at some meeting or something. Come on in and we'll have dessert together. Hope you like lemon meringue pie. It's all I've got."

"Lemon's fine. In fact it's great, it's my favorite."

The two men sat at the dining room table and quietly ate pie, washing it down with coffee. Trent got up to put his dish in the sink and poured more coffee.

"What's on your mind?" Trent asked.

Ken explained that for reasons he couldn't discuss, he had to get out of Riverside Dreams. He had to sell, but couldn't absorb the loss. This wasn't true but he wouldn't be able to sell at any price and he couldn't afford the loss of the entire house.

"Not much of a market out there, you sell now, you're going to take a bath."

"Any suggestions."

Trent looked up at the ceiling as if expecting to see an answer up there. Next, he went over to a small desk and opened the middle drawer and reached in.

Ken figured he had some fantastic papers in there. Something that would magically make his problems disappear. Some legal trick that only Trent knew about.

Trent reached in, took out a small object and tossed it to Ken. Ken looked down and on the cover of a book of matches that was emblazoned, 'Tammy the Tremendous Tassel Twirler—Appearing Nightly at Tidily Winks Roadhouse.'

What the hell is this a joke? Maybe Tammy is an entrepreneur who buys out lost causes?

"First, make sure your insurance is paid up and in effect. Make sure you have sufficient fire coverage and apply one of those," he pointed to the matches, "very carefully to the interior. Put it near an electrical appliance and don't use any fire starter or gasoline."

"Like hell, I don't want to spend my retirement in jail."

"Hey, it's done all the time. Only the real numb nuts get caught. Only about twenty percent of arsonists get caught. Not much arson going on around here—yet—but don't wait too long. The real estate market the way it is, it's only a matter of time. When it becomes popular, the fire inspectors will catch on, so if you're going to do it, do it real soon. Besides if you have to do time, you're so old no cell mate will be interested in you."

The scene from "*Fletch*" in which Chevy Chase is thrown into a jail cell with Randall "Tex" Cobb flashed through Ken's mind.

Chapter 33

Orfeo Gasparilla—he was calling himself Gasparilla now. If anyone looked at him strangely when he mentioned his name, he claimed Jose Gaspar was his great-grandfather and his real name was Jose Orfeo Gaspar, but they could call him Orfeo because he used the name Gasparilla only on special occasions.

He also told a tale about how his great friend Fabricio Chávez had been eaten by a huge Hammerhead Shark while the two were diving for treasure off the coast of Boca Grande. He thought this story and a shark was far more romantic sounding than the fact Fabio had been eaten by some crummy alligator in the murky waters of the Ocklawaha.

Orfeo had given up his digs at near the Riverfront Dreams development and had returned to his shack on a sand road near Lady Lake. By this time he had nearly forgotten the Sheriff might be looking for him and wasn't nearly as concerned about being 'captured.'

His newfound feelings of self-worth prompted him to begin fixing up his home. He gave it a new coat of paint and patched the tin roof. Inside, he painted and replaced some furniture. All of this was paid for, not by panhandling, but by odd jobs he picked up from time to time.

Every day, Orfeo returned to his nest near the old cypress tree to see if there was any new activity that he should be aware of. He noted that the two *gringos* had not returned since the smaller gator had been killed and taken away.

* * * *

"Hey Ken, get down to the laundry room and take a look. I think *your* Riverfront Dream is sliding into the river. Maybe I should say Riverfront Nightmare," Rayna chided."

"Yes dear, I'll get on it right away."

Ken was on it. He had checked and double-checked the insurance policy. He would have moved on his plan sooner, but he was awaiting a propitious moment, a moment when he would have the nerve to strike a match. He had to arrange for Rayna to be away. He didn't want her involved, so the less she knew, he better.

The arrangements were all in place. Rayna was visiting a sister at Hilton Head and Ken had decided the laundry room was the place to start. There was no insulation or drywall over the dryer, so a good hot fire should burn through the ceiling and quickly spread through the house. The house wasn't really close to any others, so the fire shouldn't be detected until things were well on their way. The Fire Department should arrive just in time to save the slab.

With a box of flammable clothing on top of the dryer, a fire starting there would appear to originate from a clogged dryer vent.

After he placed a lighted match in the bottom of the box, Ken left the house and went to a theater at the Leesburg Lakeside Mall to catch the 7:30 movie. Before he left, he researched the movie on the Internet in the event that some future investigator might ask his whereabouts the night his house burned.

He killed time after the movie, went to an all-night diner for coffee and pie and looking at his watch, determined enough time had elapsed so that he would be able to arrive at his house in time to see the fire trucks rolling up their hoses and packing away air tanks in preparation for leaving Riverfront Dreams.

* * * *

Sirens were screaming outside as Ken awakened in a strange place and someone was knocking at the door. He threw on a robe and answered the door. Outside was a man in uniform who was asking to come in. He sounded very strange, almost as if he was in the bottom of a barrel.

"You Mr. Kenneth ahh, Piccard?"

"Yeah, what can I do for you?"

"Where is Mrs. Piccard?"

"She's out of town, visiting her sister, why? Something wrong?"

"Just checking. I'm going to have to take you downtown for questioning," the man replied.

"Questioning? For what?"

"I think you know."

"About the fire?"

"Yes, about the fire. It would go a lot easier if you cooperate. We know the fire is arson and we know you started it. So, make it easy on yourself and come along."

"I didn't do it. I'm innocent. I want to call a lawyer."

"We already called Ambrogino Bellucci."

How in the hell do they know about him, Ken asked himself.

"Put your clothes on and I'll snap these cuffs on you. You'll probably have to spend the rest of the night in the slammer."

A jail cell with Randall "Tex" Cobb smiling through lipstick painted lips came to Ken once again, only this time it was real and three-dimensional. But everything seemed out of kilter somehow. *What cop would call a holding cell 'the slammer?'*

Ken awakened in a very real cold sweat in the Waterfront Motel in Lady Lake. He recalled going to the house and seeing the burned out shell. The concrete and stucco structure had survived but it was a cracked and gutted wreck—a total loss. The firemen told him to find lodging for the night and to call his insurance company and the Fire Marshal in the morning.

He remembered checking in to the motel and falling exhausted, into bed. He vaguely remembered a dream about someone knocking on the door. He punched the wall to see if it was real. It was real enough to bruise his fist and make a dent in the wall.

* * * *

The investigation was a *pro forma* affair. Ken and Rayna could tell the Fire Marshal was going through the motions. He wanted to get paid for doing his job, file some papers and be on his way. It was no skin off of his butt even if it was arson. If he had some kind of definite proof, if the arsonist had been a pro, he might even have a clue or two. As it was, the homeowner didn't have a blemish on his record and he was a plain vanilla senior, upstanding, citizen—not a candidate for any sort of further investigation. The worst scenario was he accidentally burned the place, a case of negligence. A very hard case to prove in this instance.

"It will probably be a while until you receive a settlement, Mr. and Mrs. Piccard, but I'm going to pass your claim on to your insurance agent. Any further questions and you can refer them to him," said the Fire Marshal with a degree of finality.

There was no way Ken was going to rebuild, particularly now that he knew the original house was built on what was essentially muck fill. Moreover there was no way he was going to get involved with the Association again.

Why didn't I burn the sucker much sooner?

"What do we do now," asked Rayna.

"Elementary my dear Rayna," said Ken, "we sell the lot. We might not get much, but whatever it is, it will be gravy— and considering we don't have to spend the rest of our lives in Riverfront Hell, it's a bargain."

Chapter 34

"RIVERFRONT LOT FOR SALE BY OWNER," read the sign. Below it was a phone number to call.

"Imagine that, nobody home, no home, just a lot with a burned out shell," said Zack to Cuss.

"How much you think they're asking?" said Cuss to no one in particular.

"Call the number and ask."

"What?"

"Call 'em up and ask how much they want for it. You ain't going to buy it, so it don't matter."

"What makes you so sure I'm not interested in buying it?" asked Cuss.

"You ain't got no money. I'd say that was my first clue. My second clue is you got no use for the lot—right?"

"Not so fast my friend. I have a use for the land. Moreover, I have a way to make a down payment on it."

"Yeah?"

"Yeah! I got a boat that's worth… uh… maybe $50k. I could get a loan for a down payment against the Miss Pent and the lot itself would be collateral."

"Okay, I'll bite, what do you want with a worthless lot in a housing development. You looking to build a retirement home?"

"Zack, I love you like a brother, but you can't seem to think any further than where your next beer is coming from. I'm going to buy that lot so I can own that old cypress tree in the back yard. So we can get down there and get that cask out without having to sneak around too much. We'll be doing some improvements—bring in a backhoe if we have to. We'll have a cover for getting the treasure out of there. We may even have a legal claim on the loot."

"Oh."

"Hell man, think of it as an investment, a few thousand for millions. Hey, I'm not going to rush in and by a pig in the poke. I'm not trusting your psychic skills, I'm going to ask for an thorough examination of the property—including that big tree down at the end of the driveway."

With that Cuss turned the truck around and headed back to their trailer home.

*   *   *   *

The new Jose Orfeo Gaspar had been watching Cuss and Zack from his riverside nest while they discussed the for sale sign in Ken's yard. He couldn't hear much of the conversation, but he had a suspicion the two men were the same ones who were messing around the tree earlier and he felt they weren't interested in the tree, they were after *his* treasure.

*   *   *   *

"Why don't you just call from here? The cell will work here as well as out there at the trailer. Besides the aluminum wall will block the signal and it's not near as good," said Zack.

"I need to sit down and think this through. I think better when I'm not driving and talking on the damned cell phone. It's no wonder people have all the wrecks they do, trying to talk or text while they are driving."

When they got back to the trailer, Cuss went inside, pulled out a sheet of paper and began to doodle. He wrote, made circles around words, connected them with lines and arrows then tore up the paper and got a new sheet.

After a couple of hours, he felt he was ready to make the call. He checked his watch and noted it was after 5:00 and decided it was too late to call. He would put it off until after morning coffee when his head would be clearer.

The next morning Cuss made the call and arranged to meet Ken for a 'tour' of the property. He told Zack that he wanted to meet the owner alone and that the fish were biting so he should go fishing for the day.

*   *   *   *

"I really never expected that you would be interested in the lot," said Ken.

"I didn't like the house all that much, but I really, really like the property. I've been looking for a waterfront lot for years. You understand that the house is now a liability and will have to be razed. That can be real expensive, especially when you have to dump the debris somewhere," said Cuss.

"I understand that so I'm not asking an arm and leg for it. I just want to get out from under it and move back north."

"So, how much are you asking?"

"I'll tell you what, you're the first guy who looked at it, so you have virgin, so to speak. I'll make you a great price if you pay all the closing costs and tie up the loose ends. I want out of here in the worst way. Every day I hang around, I'm paying rent, so you've got me. Make an offer."

"No, no, no, I don't work that way. You give me at least a starting point and we can haggle from there. I find out how badly you want to sell and you find out how badly I want it," said Cuss, trying to keep the tone light and friendly.

"I looked at some lots out on the lake and they are selling for big bucks, so I figure with the demolition costs and all, fifty thousand is a fair price."

"Okay."

"What?"

"It's a fair price. I thought I might have to sell my boat or borrow the money from somewhere, but I have almost that amount in my savings account. If you can take forty-eight, it's a deal. I have enough in checking to cover closing and I can wait a while before demolition. What do you think?"

Ken paused for about three beats before he blurted out, "You got a deal." He extended a hand and the deal was struck.

"You understand the deal is contingent upon inspection," Cuss said.

"What, you mean I'm going to have to wait until some bureaucrat from some state office gets around to inspecting it. I don't think—."

"You worry too much, I just want to check some things out for myself. Shouldn't take much more than an afternoon. Is that okay?"

"I… uh… I suppose so," Ken said apprehensively and stuck out his hand once more."

"I'll be back with my buddy tomorrow, give her the once over and we'll get this deal out of the way by the middle of next week."

Ken was filled with anxiety about the 'inspection.' He couldn't imagine what he might be inspecting for on an empty lot. Maybe he would learn about the lot being on unstable fill and back out of the deal. He sure didn't feel like celebrating yet.

Cuss and Zack returned the next day and parked the pickup in the driveway. The sky was overcast and a light drizzle had begun as a cold foreboding closed in on the two men.

"It's got a bad feel to it," aid Zack.

"Don't start with that psychic crap on me now. So it's not warm and sunny and you're not bright-eyed and bushy-tailed. What else is new?"

"Let's get this over with," said Zack as he got a dive mask, a snorkel and some sneakers out of the back of the pickup. "No need for fins on this one, too shallow."

"You going in?" said Cuss as Zack sat down on the asphalt

and removed his shoes and trousers. He had swimming shorts underneath, so he was ready to get into the water.

"Make like it's Spring Bayou and you're going in after that cross," said Cuss.

"Hey, it's cold enough here today without reminding me of that. That's some cold water."

"Poor baby. Should have brought him a wet suit so he would be nice and comfy."

The water looked awfully murky and one wouldn't think anyone could see more than a foot. However, the clarity of the water was an illusion created by the color of the bottom mixed with particles hanging in it. Visibility was actually closer to three or four feet.

"Take this with you," Cuss said, handing him a four-foot steel tipped pole. "You run into any turtles, gars or gators, it might come in handy."

"Thanks for reminding me what's in the river. Now I'm getting more than cold feet—or should I say cold ass."

Zack was now up to his butt in the water as he took the pole. He bent down and spit into his mask and rinsed it in river water to keep it from fogging up in the cold. He secured his snorkel through the mask strap, blew a breath of air through it and laid out on the surface. Cuss heard a sort of moan through the snorkel as Zack became accustomed to the cold water.

Long years of diving blessed Zack with an amazing lung capacity so Cuss wasn't at all concerned when Zack went beneath the surface for three minutes at a time.

When he surfaced from one of his dives of only a few feet, Cuss said, "You got that crap pretty much stirred up by now. You see anything down there?"

Zack ignored the question for the present and made his way to the shore before he removed the mask and snorkel and blew his nose.

"It's down there alright. Right where I thought it would be. That old gator had quite a dugout made for himself. I went back in there for a minute or two for a look around. I couldn't tell if it's a cask or a chest, too cloudy, but it's there. Not all that big, like I said, about the size of a nail keg."

"You think it will be hard to get it out?"

Zack was now standing and shivering. "Ain't gonna' be that easy. Might have to get a long-reach backhoe in and I know how you'd hate doing that. I'll go down and tie a marker buoy to the spot where it lies."

Chapter 35

Now more excited about the prospect now that he thought he and Zack were really onto something, Cuss called Ken and told him the inspection was positive and the deal could go forward.

"I'm leaving that all up to you," said Ken. "Give me a cashier's check for the agreed upon amount, let me sign off where necessary and I'm outta' here."

Cuss made a quick call to his attorney in Key West who turned him onto a buddy in Ocala. Within a matter of hours, the attorney had drawn up a sales agreement and all of the subsequent papers that would be needed. It wasn't as fast as the Riverside Dreams developers' closing, but it moved along very quickly. Within a few days Cuss was given the rights to the property, at least until the closing could be accomplished. Ken signed a power of attorney with a local attorney and turned the transaction over to her.

Cuss believed he might be able to move in a backhoe, get the loot out and abandon the deal before he had to put any more than earnest money down. He was far more anxious to dump five thousand into the deal than the full amount of the sale. After all, all he needed was time to get the cask into the truck and be on his way.

He contacted Sunshine Equipment Rentals in Ocala and arranged to have a hoe delivered to the property within one week. The day-rate was reasonable and he had no reason to believe he would need it for more than a day. He was filled with anticipation as he looked at the spot where a little yellow marker was floating.

The backhoe arrived on a heavy hauler and pulled into the access road in front of what was now Cuss's lot. In the middle of the unloading of the machine, Larry Winters appeared at the top of the drive.

"Stop right there," Winters commanded. "What the hell do you think you are doing?"

"Unloading this here equipment," replied the driver. "What's it look like."

"You don't have permission from the Association," claimed Larry.

"No, but I've got this here delivery order and that's all I need," said the driver as he climbed onto the bed and began unloading the backhoe while Winters blustered fussed and fumed.

"Get that damned thing out of there," demanded Winters.

"You'll have to talk with the property owner. He gives me an order to remove it, I remove it, that's the only way it's going to happen."

The driver climbed into the cab of the truck and drove off, leaving an apoplectic Larry Winters standing shaking his fist at the departing vehicle.

A day later, Cuss, who had some experience with hydraulic lifting equipment and Zack who had experience helping around it, returned to tackle the job of removing the cask.

"I think you're going to have to remove some of the roots and knees around it, then I can get a strap on it and you should be able to lift it right out and swing it onto the bank," advised Zack.

"Let's see if we can expedite things and get the job done before someone else comes along," said Cuss.

About this time, Larry Winters pulled into the driveway.

"What's up?" Cuss asked congenially, not expecting a confrontation.

"You're going to have to get that thing out of here."

"Who says?"

"Look, I'm the president of the Riverfront Dreams Home Owners Association. I say you have to vacate these premises right now."

"How about giving me a break. I just have to take down the rest of that burned out wreck, it will only take a half-day and it will make this development look one heck of a lot better," Cuss said, hoping to defuse the situation.

"Can't. Gotta' go by the rules. The rules say any demolition has to be approved by the Board. You are going to have to submit a plan to the Association and the Board will have to approve it."

"I have a permit for demolition from Lake County, it's approved and signed and everything," Cuss lied.

"That's nice, good to see you like following rules," Winters said in a snide tone. "But that don't cut no ice around here. You gotta' have *Board* approval. It shouldn't hold you up much, we have a meeting next month."

"So long as your Association has a good liability policy. That wreck over there is a glaring safety hazard. Anyone gets hurt here and any attorney right out of school will make mincemeat of your members. Of course *I* would never make a formal complaint, but someone with a beef against the Association—."

At this point Larry's body language gave him away. He stared out at the river in deep thought. He knew he was going to have to allow the men access. If he gave in, his ego would take a beating. If he didn't the Association might be on the hook for damages.

"Tell you what, come to the office and fill out a permission to demolish form and a form that releases us from liability and I'll let you go ahead and take that building down. Now that's fair, isn't it?"

* * * *

Jose Orfeo Gaspar—or Gasparilla if you will—was nearby listening to the whole confrontation. He could barely contain himself and held his hand over his mouth to stifle his laugh. He had seen enough of the honcho *jefes* like Larry Winter to last a lifetime and enjoyed every minute of seeing him have to come to an agreement with the other Gringo.

* * * *

After the permission formalities, Cuss and Zack returned to the job at hand. Zack donned his dive mask, snorkel and tennis shoes and began the task of fastening a chain to a big root. Now intent on, and distracted by, the work at hand, he didn't notice the ripples being pushed his way.

Cuss drove the backhoe down the driveway and as close to the water's edge and cypress tree as he dared. Too close and he'd be hung up in the muck, too far away and the hoe would be ineffective. At the farthest point, he began to feel the backhoe sink into the riverbank. He backed up a little and waited to see if he was on firm ground.

Cuss looped the chain around the bucket of the hoe and fastened it with a clevis. Thus secured, he pulled the chain taught to check to see if it was fastened on the other end, mounted the cab of the machine and rather than try to lift the root, he backed up until he reached the pavement of the driveway and began pulling the massive root behind him. It snapped loose with a fearsome tug and was deposited on the riverbank.

While Zack regained the chain, Cuss used the boom and bucket on the backhoe to maneuver the root to a resting place on the riverbank.

"Any more stuff we have to get out of the way down there?" asked Cuss.

"We'll have to wait for the water to clear so I can get a good look, but I think that should do it."

The drizzle had cleared, and by now a couple of Riverfront Dreams residents had taken up places on the river bank near the recovery site. One even brought along a lawn chair. Another observer, Orfeo Gaspar, was ensconced in his lookout post some distance away.

"Don't look much like they're demolishing the place to me," said the first resident to the one sitting in the lawn chair.

"Is that what their supposed to be doing?" asked the guy in the lawn chair.

"Larry Winters gets wind of this, he'll be down here and put a stop to it. Looks to me like they're just making a big mess."

"Hey, hey," shouted the lawn chair guy.

Perturbed to be interrupted, Cuss turned his attention to the kibitzers. "What?"

"I thought you guys were to raze the burned out building. What are you doing in the river? Don't you know you can get into all kinds of environmental trouble doing that kind of thing?"

Cuss thought for a moment about what kind of convincing story he might tell they men.

"We're down here to tear down the house, but the Water Authority asked us to clean out a place where they intend to put a monitoring station. We're doing them a favor. We ain't getting paid diddly for doing it either. Saving you guys tax money to boot. We'll be glad to quit and let the H.O.A. pick up the tab if you like."

"Oh. Well I suppose we don't want to interfere with progress or anything like that."

"You guys know where we might dump some of the junk we might find in there? You know how it is getting rid of debris anymore."

"No, just don't dump it around the development."

"Yeah, said the guy without a chair. "Just put it in your pickup and take it to a landfill. They may charge a fee, but it will be a lot cheaper than a fine if you just dump it."

"The man says haul it away," Cuss said to Zack who returned a big grin.

"We can do that," said Zack who by now had moved back to the water's edge in preparation to put a three-inch-wide nylon strap around the cask so he could attach he chain to it. The plan was to lift the object straight up, back the hoe up the driveway and swing it around until the boom was over the truck bed and drop the cask in the pickup.

We'll be lucky if that thing doesn't break open and dump whatever is inside. Wouldn't that be just great, a fortune in gold spread out in public view.

Chapter 36

Zack returned to the task of rigging the cask. Once again there was a slight ripple behind him. Behind the ripple were two nostrils barely above the surface and a full eighteen inches behind the nostrils were a set of black pupils that looked like vertical slits against a light green eyeball protruding above the water. If Zack had been more aware of his surroundings, he would have seen those malevolent eyes reflected and barely distorted in the rippling water. The ripples formed a 'V' with the point of which was directed straight at Zack.

Totally preoccupied with the work of recovering the cask, Zack had neglected to bring along the steel-tipped rod with him. He was lulled into a sense of confidence; safe in the knowledge the 'big gator' had been removed and killed. Little did he realize that there was a reptilian beast fully six feet longer than the one that had been killed. He had no idea that this gator was a record-setter for the State, larger than Lake Weir's Old Joe. He was seven inches longer than the State record gator.

Cuss was busily finishing attaching the chain to the

backhoe in preparation for lifting the cask and not paying much attention to what was going on in the river.

On the bank, the two men had become bored with the work at hand and were shooting the breeze. Only Orfeo was aware of the attack about to take place at the edge of the Ocklawaha.

Casually, almost gently the immense reptile turned sideways, as might a shark and took Zack's leg in his jaws. It was as if he were delicately sampling a hors d'œuvre. Instinctively Zack knew his attacker was behind him and with all his might, without turning, he slammed the beast in the eyes with the chain. The chain wrapped around his head in a maneuver an oilfield roughneck might call 'throwing the chain' around a drill pipe.

Zack screamed for help as the gator frantically struggled to be free. Cuss heard the scream and intuitively threw the hydraulic lever to raise the backhoe's long boom. For what seemed like minutes, the gator hung suspended and flailing over the river while Zack managed to get to shore with the help of the two Riverfront residents.

As soon as Zack managed to get out of the water, the gator freed himself from the entangling chain and plopped back into the river. Once he got his bearings, he sped off downriver in a northerly direction. This time, there was no giant circular route back home; he was well on his way toward the Route 42 Bridge.

Zack was bloodied, but unbowed—almost unperturbed. The bite he received was more of a scraped bruise and wouldn't require stitches, only some antiseptic and a bandage. He even refused to go to the emergency room at the local hospital.

"Close call," said Orfeo who had left his hideaway and joined the men at the riverbank. "You probably ain't going to see that one again for quite a while."

"I'm glad you think so, but I'm not so sure," said Zack.

"Oh, he be gone alright. May never come back here now, you can be sure."

"If you're so damned sure, why don't you go down and finish hooking up that chain?" Almost as an afterthought, Zack added, "Who the hell are you anyway."

Orfeo stood a tall as he could, puffed out his chest and announced, "I am Jose Orfeo Gaspar THE Gasparilla."

"Cuss stifled a laugh, but Zack let his out. "I'll bet you're that pirate fella' from down at Tampa aren't you. You escape from the parade or something?" said Zack in as sarcastic a tone as he could muster.

"No *mi amigo*, I am not the pirate, that was my great grandfather, Jose Gaspar. I am THE living Gasparilla, come to help you in your hour of need—sent by God himself. You my friend don't know it, but you were delivered this day from the ghost of the pirate Gasparilla." Orfeo crossed himself. "*In nomine Patris et Filii et Spiritus Sancti.*"

Zack was speechless until he thought of something to say. "Amen *amigo*."

"Now, if someone has a crucifix, I will enter the waters and attach the chain to the object beneath the surface. You may stay here on shore safe and secure."

Damian Zanakias had worn a golden miniature replica of the Epiphany Cross of Spring Bayou around his neck on a gold chain for decades. He had never removed it until this day. Today he reached into his shirt and carefully took the chain from around his neck and offered it to THE Gasparilla.

"Here, my friend, take this with my blessing. I only hope it provides you the same protection it gave me today," said Zack.

Without so much as a furtive glance, Orfeo entered the Ocklawaha and with no dive mask or snorkel he disappeared beneath the murky water and then rose again, holding the cross on high.

"The chain is attached and you may lift the object free. *Dios bendice esta tarea.*" *This must be the way it felt to be El Lector,* thought THE Gasparilla.

Cuss once again lifted the boom. Beneath it dangled a muddy blob wrapped in yellow belting. He held his breath as he backed up the driveway toward the burned out house and rotated the boom and dropped the blob into the bed of the pickup truck. The truck groaned and its springs compressed under the load, the old oak container had held together. Zack scrambled aboard the truck, loosened the binding and rolled the muddy object into the front of the truck and chocked it in place with a piece of timber.

With Orfeo still in tow, Cuss called Sunshine Equipment Rentals and told them the machine was ready to be picked up. He gave his home and his Key West Bank address as the place to send his deposit. Although he wasn't the best penman in the world, Orfeo memorized the address until he could write it down.

"What do I owe you?" Cuss asked Orfeo. "I don't think I could have talked Zack into going back in that river, and I know, for a fact, sure as hell, I wasn't going to do it either."

"*It's nada,*" said Orfeo. "It was my pleasure to be of service—of help—to you. You might say it is an obligation of being the Gasparilla. It was something I *must* do."

"You got any cash on you?" Cuss asked Zack.

"Yeah, a couple hundred, I reckon, why?"

"Give."

Zack handed two wrinkled and damp bills to Cuss who added a couple more to the amount. "Here, at least take this," he said handing the money to Orfeo.

"NO! I would be offended to take it. I appreciate the offer, but no, it wouldn't be right."

Cuss carefully folded the bills and tried to stuff them into Oreo's pocket. He moved at the last minute and the bills fell to the ground. Cuss didn't notice and jumped into the truck, asked Zack to get in and began to drive off.

"Un momento, un momento," shouted Orfeo as he handed the crucifix to Cuss. "This belongs to him," he said nodding in Zack's direction.

Zack replied, "You keep it. It's gold, worth two thousand dollars at least. You keep it—please.

Orfeo replied with one word, "*Nunca.*" And walked away.

As he passed nearly five hundred dollars laying on the ground, he went out of his way to walk over and grind his heel into the bills.

"The damned yanqui gringos, they steal my gold, the gold of my ancestors and try to give me nickels and dimes for it. The Gasparilla does not take such an insult easily."

Chapter 37

Near Homestead, Florida, Quinn Kussler and Damian Zanakias pulled into a self-service car wash to clean the mud and debris of the Ocklawaha from their pickup.

Ignoring a sign which cautioned, "NO CLEANING TRUCK BEDS," and without at thought to the relic in front of him, Zack turned the pressure spray onto the football shaped object in the truck bed. He was careful to keep the high-pressure spray from damaging the soft wood of the shell that he believed to contain a fortune in silver and/or gold. It never occurred to either of them at this point that the cask itself might be valuable.

The keg was about two feet long and approximately 12 inches wide or sixteen inches in diameter. Neither Zack nor Cuss had any idea about the weight or what was in the container. They were apprehensive of any attempt to lift it for fear it would fall apart. After a good washing, it did look a bit more like a treasure or wine cask.

Actually the men were perhaps more apprehensive that it was indeed a wine or rum keg and it would contain nothing more than sand, mud and water.

With the truck and treasure cleaned up, the couple headed on down Route 1, the Overseas Highway. Hopping from bridge to key to bridge again. Zack slept in the passenger's seat while Cuss concentrated on driving. Neither of them gave a thought to the scenery or the legacy of Henry Morrison Flagler whose railroad bridges gave birth to the highway they were traveling on.

"Well, I'm waiting," said Zack.

"For what, you need to stop this is a hell of a place for it."

"I'm waiting for you—"

"Unless you tell me what for, you're going to have a very long wait," Cuss interrupted.

"You know, the apology."

"What? Your mind slip a cog?"

"You doubted that we would find the treasure, now it's in the back of your pickup and you're on your way home. Now let's hear it from Mr. No Imagination," said Zack, smugly.

"Okay, okay, I admit you are a psychic genius and I humbly beg your pardon, Mr. Wizard," replied Cuss, overflowing with sarcasm.

"You wanted and extra seventy-five bucks if we didn't find it. I want seventy-five for finding it. And—don't say something you wouldn't say in front of your mother or priest."

Home was a half of a duplex rental at 1711 Petronia Street close to Garrison Bight. The rental was an absolute dump when Cuss had moved in. It was still pretty much a dump, but now it was worth more than ten times what the landlord had paid for it. The rent had gone up consistently with the value and the cost of real estate taxes.

They pulled into a small alley then to a short inlet off the street. "Well, this is it, home sweet home," said Cuss.

"You want to open it up right away, or wait a while?" asked Zack.

"I'm going to walk to the variety store and pick up a cheap tarp. We'll just cover it for now. Don't want to attract too much attention. Tomorrow we'll get some tools and open the thing up."

"Good idea," said Zack, "all the pirates aren't just the past history of the Keys. Now they are on crystal meth and horse, looking for a way of funding their next fix."

After a fitful night's sleep Zack and Cuss went to the truck and rigged the tarp to form a tent over the truck bed. The purpose of the tent was to shield their activities from curious passersby. They gathered some tools, a hammer, a chisel, a pry-bar, vise-grips and a big common screwdriver.

"How you gonna' go about this? I'd like to save the cask if we can. It's got to be valuable as a collectible," said the penurious Zack.

"I think we can get the top—or bottom—whatever, off and go from there."

"Any idea which is the top?"

"No, but I guess one end is as good as another," Cuss

said, as he turned the heavy object up in a vertical position to examine the edges of the top/bottom head of the thing. His main concern was accidentally breaking the hoops holding it together. They were fashioned of brass or some other copper alloy and the staves were held together more by force of habit than by compression.

Cuss felt around the chime, the groove carved around the top of the staves to hold the head in place. He didn't find a notch or a place where he could put a pry-bar. He tapped the head gently with the hammer, not gently enough however and it cracked and a gap appeared between the boards that made up the head. From that point on, it was a simple matter to take the pieces of the head out one by one. The cask was open at what proved to be the top.

"Can you see anything in there?" asked Zack apprehensively.

"What did you expect, shiny coins? Alls I can see is sand and muck. Get the garden hose and turn just a trickle of water on at the tap."

Cuss directed the small stream into the cask and began washing away the mud and grit. When it seemed it would take forever to flush the dirt away, he gently reached in and began to take out material by hand.

* * * *

Orfeo went to his shack on the sand road not far from the housing development and went to the place he had hidden his Glock. He decided he would need money to finance any move against the Anglo thieves. He had never been a man of violence and he told himself his petty crimes were few and mainly for necessities that he required in order to live.

He convinced himself he was not a criminal and in this case he was justified. His robbery would be against the white skinned devils who were the same as those who had stolen what was really his. It was no crime to take back that which had been stolen—that which was his. To him, it wasn't a racist act. Many Anglos had befriended him and he felt close to many of them. This was a case of *venganza*, a case of honor.

Wearing a straw hat and posing as a gardener, Orfeo found himself exploring houses in one of the middle class retirement communities in the area. He found one that appeared to be an excellent choice. There were papers on the porch that suggested the residents had been away for at least four days. There was no yapping dog and an examination of the sliding doors leading in from the deck led him to believe it would be easy pickings.

By tugging on the door handle, Orfeo learned that the lock, like most sliding door locks, no longer functioned and managed to pull the door aside far enough to cause a small slot to open. Next, using a steel blade, he, with some difficulty lifted the safety bar that had been dropped into place to lock the door. The sliding door bar was a common device used by unsuspecting homeowners. No one really believed that someone would have the nerve to invade a home in their own tightly knit community.

He bypassed the valuable electronics and the computer sitting on a desk. He was looking for cash. Something he would not have to pawn, something that wouldn't draw attention to him. After pulling out and dumping the contents of nearly every dresser draw in the place it occurred to him to pull out the drawer at the computer desk. It contained no money either. Almost as an afterthought, he turned it over and was thrilled by the sight. There was a large manila envelope taped to the bottom of the drawer with duct tape.

A hasty examination of the envelope proved it was filled with hundred-dollar bills. There were at least thirty or perhaps fifty of them; he didn't take the time to count. He carefully closed the door so that it would appear from the outside the house was undisturbed and beat a hasty retreat back to his shack.

The man at Tienda La Jimenez was pissed off because Orfeo had handed him a hundred-dollar bill for a Baby Ruth candy bar and asked for a dollars worth of quarters as well.

The store clerk held the bill to the light and marked it with counterfeit detector pen. He wrinkled and straightened it, almost refusing to believe it was real and reluctantly handed Orfeo his change.

Orfeo knew he would never be able to take his pistol aboard a commercial airline flight and he knew it might be essential in any confrontation with the Key West Gringos. He went to a pay phone outside the door of the Teinda and dropped some quarters in the slot and while he dialed the number for an airplane charter service he had found in a phone book. The service was on the Gulf Coast near Crystal River. He absent-mindedly scraped something from the chrome front of the phone with a yellowed thumbnail while he awaited an answer.

"Hello," came a female voice in the phone's receiver.

"This is Orfeo Gaspar." He chose to forgo the Gasparilla part because it might cause confusion, never mind a loss of credibility.

"Aero-Mech. How may I help you Mr. Gaspar?"

"I need to rent… charter a plane to Key West."

"That's pretty expensive, it's almost a five-hundred mile trip."

"Please understand, that isn't a problem for me. Also I need to be picked up somewhere close to Lady Lake."

"There's a landing strip call Fly Inn north of Lake Griffin. Do you know where it is?"

"I thinks so; I'll find it."

"It's going to be an additional hundred and thirty dollars to pick you up."

"As I said," said Orfeo, trying to sound more important than he felt, "money is no object. Tell you what, if you can pick me up in two hours and get me to Key West this afternoon, I'm prepared to pay you double your usual amount—in cash."

"That's pretty short notice but I'll try," said the woman enthusiastically.

"Try real hard, and there will be a two-hundred dollar gratuity in it just for you."

"I'm placing the flight request right now. Do you have a credit card?"

"Oh yes," Orfeo lied. "I have it right here—somewhere." He waited a few seconds then told the woman he couldn't locate it.

"I can't very well place an order if you can't substantiate payment. The total will come to two-thousand, one-hundred and thirty dollars."

"I'll pay the pilot in cash."

"And what happens if I send a pilot and plane out there and you don't show up?"

"Are you a *jugador*—a gambler?"

"That's got nothing to do—"

"A five-hundred dollar gratuity for a roll of the dice. It's a better offer than you will get at the Seminole Hard Rock, or the dog track. What do you say? The most you got to lose is a few minutes of airtime. Come on, roll the dice."

It never dawned on Orfeo that he could have taken a taxi to the Fly Inn, so he walked and hitchhiked. He had about fifteen minutes to spare when he arrived at the air strip to find a Beach Bonanza sitting on the apron with its engine idling. Orfeo approached the plane as the pilot reached over and popped the passenger hatch.

"Two-thousand, one-hundred and thirty dollars," were the first words out of his mouth. "And, Janine, back at the office says you owe her five-hundred in cash."

Chapter 38

Back on Petronia Street in Key West, Zack was handing a kitchen strainer to Cuss. It was a utensil they usually used for draining water from spaghetti.

"Think that'll work?" asked Zack.

"Don't know, I'll put some of this stuff in it and you take the hose and see if the crap will drain out leaving the coins or whatever behind."

Cuss took the strainer and attempted to leave as much sand and muck behind, put a handful of dirt and small round balls into the strainer.

"I think these might be pearls," he said handing the strainer to Zack for washing.

After a few minutes of rinsing, Zack said, "The might have been pearls, but now they ain't much of anything. I think the tannic acid, pollution or whatever got to 'em."

"I think you're right," Cuss said as he picked one up to examine it. There's a layer of them, so I guess we sift through all of them. You never know."

After what seemed like eons of sifting through the crap in the cask and turning up nothing but acid etched pearls, beads—

or whatever they were—Cuss approached a layer of what appeared to be coins. Gold at last?

The next layer wasn't gold. It was silver and if the men had found it a few months earlier they would have been tickled pink with their find. But now they had their money and minds invested in a gold find. Zack grumbled as he sifted through sand and mud, pulling out antique silver coins that were worth thousands—but not millions. Next there was a jumble of silver bars and some jewelry, but no gold.

Under one of the small silver bars was a coin encrusted with some kind of corrosion, by all indications not gold, but some other non-ferrous material. To Cuss's eye, it appeared to be a coin with a hole in the center, like hundreds of others he'd seen—probably oriental in origin.

Maybe valuable to a collector, but for what we are looking for, junk.

There were handfuls of the small disks with holes in the center. Cuss tossed them into the strainer and handed the mess to Zack.

"Nothing to get excited about. Get the muck off and hand me the strainer." Cuss's heart was sinking as he was nearly halfway through the cask and there was no sign of gold.

"You want me to take over digging for a while and you get down here and rinse," offered Zack.

"You're the magic man, maybe it will change our luck. Get your butt up here, he said as he hopped off the tailgate into the driveway."

Once on the ground, Cuss grabbed the hose and waited for the next strainer full of whatever Zack scooped up.

"Have you been trying to keep things separated?" asked Cuss.

"I just threw the pearls or beads, or whatever they are, there beside the house. The silver bars and coins are in that plastic basket on your right. The other stuff is in the plastic basket on your left." The silver basket looked pitiful considering what their expectations had been.

"Get busy, there looks like something coming after I get through the things that look like brass washers." He picked up one of the small perforated disk. "Hey, you know, I think that's what they are, brass washers."

Zack handed Cuss the strainer that was filled with a mass of stuff that seemed like it was rusted together. It proved to be several hand-forged nails—or what was left of them. The next 'treasure' he rinsed was a collection of brass hinges.

"How much room is left?" he asked.

"We're about… oh… I reckon, about six inches from the bottom."

"Let me guess, nothing looks like gold."

"Not so far. You know what I think—" he continued without waiting for an answer. "I think we got a treasure trove of junk."

"I think you may be right. This stuff was probably very valuable to the guys who stole it and stashed it, though. I'll be lucky if we get enough out of this crap to cover expenses. I'm sure glad I didn't pay for that lot. My real fear in this whole deal is the realtor will track me down and demand payment for it."

"We can only hope some of it will be attractive to collectors. I don't know how much silver is bringing, but I know it's gone up recently."

"Unfortunately I do. It's bringing about twenty-five dollars an ounce. Compared to what gold is bringing, it's a pittance."

"Maybe the jewelry will be desirable and bring a big price."

"You'd better hope so. This is beginning to have the smell of loser all over it."

"I think we got something in this one," Zack said as he handed Cuss another drainer full of stuff.

"I believe you may have something. Any more of this up there?"

"That's it," he said as he carelessly turned and nearly fell over the cask which immediately fell apart leaving a lump of sand on the floor of the truck bed. He immediately ran his fingers through the small pile and turned up nothing.

"Like I said, that's it, the bottom of the barrel. What you find?"

"Two very, very small gold bars. One for each of us and maybe enough to pay for our time and trouble, but don't plan on retiring to the South Seas on it."

"Well, at least we didn't get completely skunked."

"Get something to put all this stuff in and I'll take care of the gold."

Zack returned with an empty aluminum tool case that was slightly larger than very thick brief case and began putting the junk in it. He left the silver laying on the drive for one last rinse while Cuss busied himself with reburying the treasure. He went to the rear of the house and behind one of the blocks that supported the structure; he pushed the gold bars under the soft sand.

When he returned, he told Zack to take the tool case into the house using the rear entrance. Zack picked up the case, which he estimated to be at least as heavy as bag of concrete mix, and trudged his way to the back stoop of the duplex. Somewhere near the rear of the building, Cuss told him to meet him in the TV-room with a couple of beers.

"You know, we've been at it for hours. Time sure slips away when you're having fun," Cuss said grimly. "We deserve a break—relax a while before beddy-bye time."

Chapter 39

Cuss could see that Zack was going to be some time getting into the house, so he went to the front entrance. He made a mental note to tell his partner about keeping the front door locked, particularly now that there was something to steal on the premises.

The lights weren't on and down on Duval Street tourists were walking toward Mallory Square to gather for the evening ritual of watching the sun sink into the Gulf. It must have been the light because Cuss thought he could see a little, dark man sitting on the sofa.

Holy shit, it's the guy who put the chain on the cask up in Lady Lake. What the hell is he doing here? How did he get here so fast?

"What the hell are you doing here?" asked Cuss.

"Here?"

"Yeah, here in my living room. What's this all about?"

"Oh, you mean here, right here in your living room? I was in town and I thought I'd drop by and see my old *amigos*. You remember? I know you been busy and all, but surely your remember your old friend, Orfeo Gaspar—the Gasparilla."

"Yeah, I remember," said Cuss, cautiously. "What do you want?"

"There you go. You Anglos always think someone who is paying a friendly visit wants something from you. You take life to seriously my friend."

Zack came stumbling into the room dragging the tool case along behind him.

"You need some help with that?" offered Orfeo.

"What the—"

"Say hello to our old friend THE Gasparilla," said Cuss. "He just *happened* to be in town and decided to stop in to say hello."

"Hello. No I can manage," said Zack as he put the case down beside the sofa.

Cuss said, "Bring in some beers. We'll all have one and celebrate the happy reunion,"

Zack returned from the kitchen with the beers, handed one to Cuss, another to Orfeo and took a seat beside the diminutive Cuban on the sofa.

"Good to see you again," said the ever-naïve Zack as he took a big slug from his bottle.

"You guys must live pretty well," Orfeo said as he held his bottle up. "Pacifico, I thought all Americans drank only Corona. I didn't know you could get it here," Orfeo said as if he only drank Pacifico.

"What brings you to the Key—

"Let's cut the crap," interrupted Cuss. "You know and I know you're here to try to finagle a cut of what we took out of the Ocklawaha. Right?"

Cuss didn't wait for an answer. "Since you turned down over five-hundred already, I have to assume you want a cut. You didn't come all the way down here for nickels and dimes."

"No señor, the Gasparilla does not want a *taste* of *his* treasure—what you call a cut."

"I really don't think you are in a position to make demands at this point. We aren't offering you a share, and that's that."

"Besides, even if you want a share, there ain't nothing…

"There ain't nothing you can do about it," interrupted Cuss, not wanting to reveal there wasn't much of value in the tool case.

"I was hoping you would be reasonable men, but I didn't think you would just hand over all of the treasure to a little helpless cubano." Orfeo reached under the cushion beside the one he was sitting on and drew out his pistol. "Say hello to my little helper, *señor* Glock."

"Hey, that's no solution to anything, put that thing away. Besides, you go shooting that off, the police will be here in a heartbeat."

"I don't think so. Between the backfires, fireworks and all the chickens running loose out there, what's one more bang or another? I'm a very nervous man; so don't make any quick moves. Get out your truck keys and put them on the coffee table."

Orfeo reached under the cushion again, took out a roll of very tough tape and tossed it to Zack who, amazingly enough, caught it in mid-air.

"You tape your buddy's hands over there. You don't do a good job and I'll put tape over your nose and mouth and let you smother—you got that?"

When Cuss's hands were immobilized, Orfeo ordered him to tape Cuss's ankles. Next he told Zack to begin taping his own ankles, then asked him to do the best he could on his wrists. "Use your mouth for an extra hand if you want to see the sunrise."

Orfeo checked both men to make sure the taping was adequate, put extra tape on their wrists and several wraps of tape around their mouths. Next he pulled out a length of light chain and a padlock and fasten his wrist to the tool case, much like a courier would attach a briefcase to himself. He then headed for the door and the pickup outside.

"*Buonas noches mis amigos.*"

Zack looked a Cuss, Cuss looked at Zack and Zack began to move his fingers and wrists to loosen his bonds. He was able to finally get Cuss's hands free and Cuss then pulled the tape off of his mouth.

"Holy shit! That smarts."

After several minutes of struggling both men were standing, looking at each other, grinning.

"Tell me you put the silver under the house," Cuss said to

Zack.

Zack grinned a wide grin and said, "You betcha, my momma didn't raise no fool."

They both started laughing. "Let the little greaser have the tool box. It's probably worth more than what's in it," said Zack.

"If we involve the law, we'll have a whole bunch of explaining to do, so let it go. Maybe there's enough junk in that tool case for him to fix up his house. I wouldn't want to have to carry it to the truck for what's in it."

* * * *

While not the brightest of souls, Orfeo knew that the problem with committing a crime on Key West was the get-a-way. If one stayed on the ground there was only one way out—the overseas highway—Route One.

On the other hand, there was the way he had arrived, by air. But it was far too risky to charter a plane, leaving a trail for those who were bound to follow. However, there were lots and lots of boats on the Keys.

It was getting darker and darker as Orfeo drove toward Key Largo. He believed if he stopped at one of the smaller, out-of-the way places and was careful enough, he could get away with a medium-size boat and then make his way to another key and get a larger boat that would allow him to get back up the Gulf coast. The switch of boats would further confuse anyone—the police or the two men—who might try to follow him.

Working in the dark, Orfeo managed to cut the chain holding a small run-about to a decrepit dock near Marathon Key. Since a number of boat owners leave their keys in their boats for the sake of convenience, the key was found in the ignition right where the owner's buddy could find it the next day.

Unfortunately, Orfeo had no clue where he was and of course it wouldn't have done much good if he did. Except for moonlight, it was almost pitch dark on the water. He knew he was on the left side—the Gulf side—of the highway, so, he reckoned he could stay well out from the shore and follow the lights east and north—if he didn't run aground.

The Cuban might not have realized it, but the waters around the Overseas Highway are unpredictable at best. At night they are predictable—you *are* going to run into trouble. Flats and shallows grooved by channels are the stuff of the bottom of this part of the Gulf. Fortunately, when Orfeo ran aground he was near one of the smaller keys.

He was close enough to hear the sirens of law enforcement running on the highway. Sirens in the area were common enough and it very well could have been an auto accident, but in his paranoid state, he knew they had to be looking for him.

At this point, he decided to try to get some sleep and hopefully a change in the tide would free his small craft and he would be on his way. There was little alternative. He couldn't very well wade to shore with the tool case chained to his wrist and he wasn't about to leave it.

The possibility of stealing another boat and heading out into the Atlantic had its appeal, but he didn't think he would be lucky enough to find another boat with a key in the ignition. Moreover there was no assurance that the Atlantic side wasn't at least as treacherous as the Gulf.

Orfeo awoke to find his boat floating free only about two hundred feet from what appeared to be a private dock. The boat's owner must have been a trusting soul because it also contained two five-gallon containers of fuel. After topping off the fuel tank, he gave the engine a try. It started and he continued cautiously on his way, steering what he believed to be east and north. Since he had no wish to be spotted, he stayed well off the coast, barely keeping some landmarks in sight.

After about a half-hour of running he was gaining confidence in his ability to navigate the waters and was well out to sea. He had not seen one boat since early morning and began to worry that they were keeping off the water because of storm warnings. His storm warning fears were allayed, but new fears set in as he saw what looked to be some kind of speedboat heading for him.

All Orfeo could think of was the sirens on the highway. *They had spotted him somehow. That new radar or something, they were on their way to arrest him.*

He tried changing course and opening up the throttle. That helped for a while but in a short while, the boat appeared on the horizon again.

"That guy's got to be up to something," said Petty Officer Jean LePhitt who was in charge of the boat out of Marathon. "Have side arms ready. If we can close on him, I intend to board and inspect that craft. Must be running dope, or he wouldn't be running from us."

Little did Orfeo know, if he had slowed down and given the Coast Guard a friendly wave, he would have easily 'escaped' his troubles. However, paranoia, driven by the fear of being arrested and sent to prison overcame reason. Seeing the Coast Guard boat closing on him, Orfeo was in a panic. Looking across the horizon for a means of escape, he headed straight toward the pass under the bridge at Conch Key. He was hoping he might lose them on the Atlantic side.

What he found on the Atlantic side was a large trackless ocean and the dogged pursuit of the Coast Guard who was now closing in fast. Within minutes he could hear the bullhorn and the officer commanding him to come about.

Panic is a sudden sensation of fear and dread that is so strong as to dominate or perhaps prevent reason and logical thinking. It consists of replacing fear with overwhelming feelings of anxiety and it is very similar to a senseless animalistic fight or flight reaction.

In a panic Orfeo locked the throttle wide open and went to the bow. Still chained to the heavy tool case, he wrapped the chain around his arm and screamed at the boat. No one on board could hear him as he shouted,

"THE GASPARILLA WILL NEVER BE TAKEN

ALIVE."

Epilogue

If there is a riverfront in heaven, Ken and Rayna Piccard may be sitting on the deck of their promised retirement mansion, looking over a blissful, heavenly version of the Ocklawaha which must have crystal clear waters even more pure than Silver Springs. They retired to where there were no homeowners associations—for eternity.

The hometown newspaper, *The Georgian Messenger* read: "Rainelle couple in fatal crash near Summersville, West Virginia. Ken and Rayna Piccard were killed instantly in a fiery crash on Wednesday morning when a logging truck crossed the median and hit their minivan head-on. They had sold their Florida residence and were returning to George County to live in retirement."

Their place on the waiting room couch was vacated while they got their ticket punched. Their daughter, who inherited the lot at Riverfront Dreams, is, to this day, trying to sell it. "Any offer considered," reads the realtor's sign.

* * * *

Who is to say if a Jose Gaspar ever walked the decks of a pirate ship? There is scant evidence that he ever existed, but don't try to sell that idea to the people of Tampa.

We do know that THE Gasparilla or what may be left of him lies somewhere off the shores of Conch Key, still attached to a tool case containing some nails, a few brass washers and some bronze hinges—at least that's what they say.

* * * *

Quinn Kussler and Damian Zanakias still live on Petronia Street in Key West. They cashed in their 'treasure' and paid some bills and deposited the rest in interest bearing accounts. Between that and Social Security they may live out their days in the sunshine. However, the dream never dies…

Daniel I. Morris is a retired college professor, newspaper publisher, artist, and writer. He lives with his wife Barbara in Southwestern Pennsylvania and they winter in central Florida—on Lake Griffin.

www.ingramcontent.com/pod-product-compliance
Lightning Source LLC
Chambersburg PA
CBHW070102260626
47160CB00004B/1285